"I was instantly immersed in the glamorous and not so glamorous world of modeling through the narration of Emerson, a heroine [who is] real and down-to-earth and completely relatable. The chemistry between Emmy and the intense but charming Ben is palpable . . . and did I mention HOT? Speaking of Ben . . . wow! Ryan does a fantastic job of bringing a male supermodel to life—Ben's the ultimate book boyfriend! Fabulous! *Working It* is a romantic and incredibly sexy read."

—Samantha Young, *New York Times* bestselling author

"*Devil Wears Prada* with a steamy twist! Grab a fan ladies, Kendall Ryan delivers a hot read that will have you begging for more."

—Molly McAdams, *New York Times* bestselling author

"Kendall Ryan's writing style is flawless. *Working It* is fast-paced and full of emotion. I couldn't put it down. Five stars all around!"

—K. A. Robinson, *New York Times* bestselling author

"Glamorous and romantic, *Working It* is the full package—a gorgeous setting, a beautiful hero, and a heroine you both root for and long to be, especially in those oh-so-sexy scenes."

—Lauren Blakely, *New York Times* bestselling author

"I LOVE the dazzling and desirable world of fashion and models. . . . This reminded me of one of my favorite movies—*The Devil Wears Prada*—but it was so much more—the emotions, the characters, and the hot factor were taken to a whole other level."

—*Shh Mom's Reading*

"*Working It* is Kendall Ryan's HOTTEST book yet. . . . The story has fabulous flow . . . Brilliant story with fantastic characters. What else could you want in a sexy read, right?"

—*Flirty and Dirty Book Blog*

"[Ben and Emmy] have some major chemistry. You can feel it. This one was hot hot hot! . . . the sex scenes were off the charts hot!"

—*Book Babes Unite*

Also by Kendall Ryan

When I Break

Working It

The Impact of You

Resisting Her

Hard to Love

Make Me Yours

Unravel Me

Craving Him

A Love by Design Novel

Kendall Ryan

ATRIA PAPERBACK

New York   London   Toronto   Sydney   New Delhi

ATRIA PAPERBACK
A Division of Simon & Schuster, Inc.
1230 Avenue of the Americas
New York, NY 10020

First Atria Paperback edition June 2014

ATRIA PAPERBACK and colophon are trademarks of Simon & Schuster, Inc.

For information about special discounts for bulk purchases, please contact Simon & Schuster Special Sales at 1-866-506-1949 or business@simonandschuster.com.

The Simon & Schuster Speakers Bureau can bring authors to your live event. For more information or to book an event contact the Simon & Schuster Speakers Bureau at 1-866-248-3049 or visit our website at www.simonspeakers.com.

Manufactured in the United States of America

10   9   8   7   6   5   4   3   2   1

Library of Congress Cataloging-in-Publication Data

Ryan, Kendall.
   Craving Him : a Love by Design Novel / Kendall Ryan.
       pages cm—(Love by Design ; 3)
Summary: "The third sexy contemporary romance novel in the Love By Design series"—Provided by publisher.
   1. Fashion—Fiction. 2. Love stories. I. Title.
   PS3618.Y3354C73 2014
   813'.6—dc23
                          2014012549

ISBN 978-1-4767-6462-7
ISBN 978-1-4767-6463-4 (ebook)

Craving Him

1

Ben

Having Emmy back in my bed was a thing of wonder. I blinked open sleepy eyes, just needing to see if it was really her next to me. Last night felt like a dream, but there she was, laying so peacefully, her cheek resting on my pillow, dark eyelashes fluttering and a mass of brown waves tangled around her face. My heart surged. She was here.

I trailed my hand lightly over her hip and backside as she lay asleep on her stomach. I loved her body . . . it was so soft, so smooth . . . it just invited my touch. Last night she'd said we'd need to go slow. But I was thankful she'd still spent the night with me. I'd never felt true peace and acceptance like I had when I was near Emmy. She accepted me for me—with her, I wasn't the man on billboards or in magazines. I was just me. Despite my shortcomings, despite all my fuck-ups, she was here by my side. After nearly losing her, I'd earned a second chance and I would do everything in my power to make things right again.

I gave her butt a gentle pat. "Wake up, baby." I should let her sleep in, relax, but I was too selfish. Knowing she was here, back in New York and back in my life, made me want to seize the day. *Carpe diem*, or some shit. I was too restless to let her sleep. We needed to make up for lost time. Now that I had her back, I wasn't going to waste a minute.

Emmy let out a small groan and stretched before rolling over toward the sound of my voice. She blinked up at me sleepily. "Morning."

"Hi." I continued letting my hand skim over her body, my fingers lightly dancing along her exposed skin where my T-shirt she'd worn to bed had ridden up. I knew I was just torturing myself. I needed to keep my hands to myself or I was going to have a massive case of blue balls later. "What do you want to do today?" I had visions of bathing her in my deep tub, taking her out for brunch at my favorite place in the city, and then maybe cuddling up in front of the fireplace later. But I was game for whatever she wanted. She would be calling the shots.

"I need to get home," she said, flinging the blankets back off her legs to climb out of bed. "I left Ellie hanging last night, and besides, I haven't been home in months."

Disappointment coursed through me. She was fleeing already. "Can I at least feed you first?" I asked, rising to stand behind her and pull her back against my chest. I couldn't resist letting my hands slide down to the curve of her hips.

"Just coffee," she murmured.

"You got it." I kissed the back of her neck and slowly released her.

While Emmy dug through her suitcase, I headed into the galley kitchen near the front of my apartment. It wasn't a room I used often. I liked to cook, but cooking for one was a waste, so I tended to order out rather than prepare a depressing meal alone. And besides, I hated doing dishes. That was why I'd hired Magda, my housekeeper. She was fabulous.

I added coffee to the machine and set it to brew. Emmy emerged a few minutes later, her hair combed and secured in a low ponytail, dressed in jeans, sneakers, and a long-sleeved tee. She looked adorable. I was going to have a hard time letting her go. Especially because she'd just returned from an extended stay in Tennessee. I'd intercepted her at the airport. My first bit of good luck since she'd left me.

When I'd told her about her boss's, Fiona's, pregnancy—possibly with my child—Emmy had quit Status Model Management without a word and fled for the comforts of home. I couldn't say I blamed her, but after running into her at the airport when returning from a shoot in Miami yesterday, and convincing her to come home with me, it seemed she was willing to give me another chance. Now that she was back, my body wanted to make up for lost time. But my heart was reminding me not to push her. I couldn't lose her again and there were a million little things I'd missed about her. I'd never felt this way about anyone before. I was desperately in love with this girl. I needed to show her that she could trust me. I wouldn't fuck this up again.

I added milk to her coffee, remembering how she liked it, and handed her the mug. "I don't even know where you live," I admitted.

She took a sip of the brew and smiled at me. "This is good coffee."

"I have it flown in from Italy."

"Wow." She took another sip. "Why don't you come over then? You can see my place and meet Ellie."

I leaned in and kissed her forehead. "Perfect. I'm going to jump in the shower and I'll give my driver a call. About fifteen minutes, okay?"

"Sounds good."

Emmy

Approaching the door to my apartment, I was a bit self-conscious for Ben to see my place. The apartment itself was located in an older run-down building in a not-so-charming neighborhood in Queens. Ellie had relocated to a cheaper unit during my absence. Compared to Ben's luxury apartment in Gramercy Park in the heart of downtown, this place was a piece. But it was all Ellie and I could afford. And it was home. For now.

Scuffed, yellowed walls and worn gray carpeting lined the narrow hallways. Green paint was peeling from our front door, and the smell of three-day-old Indian food permeated the corridor as soon as you entered the building. Charming, I know.

Ben attempted a reassuring smile as I fumbled with the key in the lock, but I could tell his eyes were assessing every detail. He'd nearly choked when I'd told the driver to head toward the Queensboro Bridge. Not all of us could afford to live in the insanely expensive heart of Manhattan like he did. I didn't know what he'd expected.

Finally freeing the second dead bolt securing the door, I pushed it open.

I'd hoped perhaps Ellie would be in her bedroom and I could have a word privately with her about Ben before he was accosted by her questions. Sadly that was not the case. Ellie was standing in the living room wearing only a towel, her hair thrown in a messy bun, mustache remover cream spread above her top lip.

She spun around, hearing our entrance. "Geez! Thanks for the warning, Em." Clutching the towel tighter to her chest, she scurried down the hall to her room.

Oops. I guess I should have texted and told her Ben and I were on our way over. I was out of practice on the etiquette of being a good roommate after living at home with my parents for the past month and alone in Paris for the two months before that.

"Sorry, Ellie!" I called out to her retreating backside. I knew she was going to be mortified that a guy as hot as Ben had seen her with depilatory cream on her face.

Ben smiled weakly. "I take it that's your roommate?"

"Yeah, that's Ellie. And I think I'm in trouble with her."

Giving Ben the grand tour took all of about three seconds. I was acquainting myself with the apartment at the same time. Dumpy living room with beige couch—*check*. Small but neatly organized kitchen—*check*. Narrow hallway leading to our bedrooms and a shared bathroom—*check*.

He smiled politely, but I knew this wasn't the type of living quarters he was accustomed to. I wondered if he'd ever stay over, or if he'd insist we stay at his place. Before I had time to ponder it further, Ellie came charging out of her bedroom.

Her eyes were bright and determined, her dark hair flowing in loose waves over her shoulders. "You," she poked Ben in the chest, "are on my shit-list."

He cocked his eyebrow up. "Uh . . . excuse me?"

"You heard me," Ellie said, her tone firm and unwavering. "I'm onto you. And Emmy will not be your plaything until you get bored. She's the fucking shit. You got that, mister?" She poked his chest one more time for emphasis before I caught her wrist and pulled it away.

"I completely agree. Emmy's the best," he said.

Ellie lifted her chin, throwing her shoulders back. "Good. We're on the same page then. But just know, I'm watching you. And I won't hesitate to kick your ass if need be."

"You're Ellie, right?" he asked.

She nodded, seeming to realize that she hadn't yet introduced herself.

Ben stepped in closer, meeting her intense gaze. "I'm going to take care of this girl. She's mine. And I'm not going anywhere."

"Okay then." Ellie's tone had softened.

My heart soared at hearing his sweet declaration.

Ellie met my eyes, looking for any signs of trouble. I kept my face neutral and gave her a small smile. She returned my grin and headed off into the living room, leaving Ben and me standing alone in the hall.

He pulled me to his chest and pressed a light kiss to my forehead.

"I'm sorry about that. She means well," I offered.

"I know, babe. No worries."

Ellie was a tough-ass New Yorker. That was for sure. She spoke her mind and didn't take crap from anyone. Apparently she was also fiercely protective of me. It was flattering and also a little bit scary.

Ben leaned down to angle his mouth against mine, kissing me tenderly. "I love you. I'm going to go so you guys catch up and talk, okay?"

"Okay. Thanks for the ride home. You didn't know you were coming all the way to Queens today, did you?"

He smiled and pressed his lips to mine once more. "Nope. But you're worth it."

He'd have a forty-five-minute subway ride back unless he called his driver again. Was that guy just at the ready, waiting for Ben's call? No time to ponder it. I walked Ben to the door. He gave a brief wave to Ellie and kissed me one last time.

"Call me later, baby."

"I will," I confirmed. My head was still reeling from the emotional weight of our reunion. I couldn't help but be both happy and apprehensive at the same time.

Closing the door behind him, I found Ellie in the kitchen, fishing a can of Diet Coke from the fridge.

"So . . ."—I leaned against the counter—"how much trouble am I in?"

Ellie straightened and popped open the top of the can,

taking a long sip. She looked me over thoughtfully. "For your supermodel boyfriend seeing me with mustache remover or for getting back together with said boyfriend in the first place?"

I smiled unevenly. "I didn't plan for this to happen. It was by complete coincidence that I ran into him at the airport yesterday. He convinced me to hear him out, and I'm glad I did. I missed him, Ellie. Like *missed* him missed him." The truth was, with our quick reunion last night, I hadn't had time to sort out all of my feelings and emotions. My heart still yearned for Ben, as foolish as it might seem. "And as for the pregnancy, that really wasn't his fault. He plans to have paternity testing done as soon as it's safe."

"And that's . . . okay with you?"

I swallowed the bitter taste in my mouth. I'd researched paternity testing extensively online and found most people waited until after the baby was born to do the test, as it was less invasive and much easier. No wonder Fiona was digging her heels in on this. I couldn't help but imagine her using any excuse to wait until after the baby was born so that, in her head, Ben could be the father a little longer. It made me sick to even think about it. Yet I clenched my jaw and nodded to answer Ellie's question.

"He's also cut off his friendship with her," I quickly added, like that made it all better somehow. I was still wary of his relationship with Fiona and knew it would take some work to rebuild my trust in him. But Ellie's constant suspicions would only make this harder. I needed to put on a brave face.

I needed to try and move past all this if he was what I really wanted.

"But he's still going to stay with her agency?" Ellie shot me a curious glare.

"Yes, for now. He's under contract." I didn't mention that this little fact also drove me mad. I didn't want him working with her, but I didn't want to give Ellie another reason to hate him, so I held my face impassive, trying to pretend it didn't bother me. That it was all just some harmless business arrangement. The truth was, I didn't trust Fiona and never would. Ben had a weakness where she was concerned, giving her too much leeway, being too accommodating.

Ellie released a deep sigh. "It killed me when you took off for home. I felt helpless and I just don't want to see you go through something like that again with him."

"It won't happen again. I'm here to stay. In fact, I need to start looking for a job so I can pay you back for rent."

Ellie waved me off. "Psshh . . . I'm not worried about the rent. I'm just glad you're back and doing well." She opened her arms. "Come here."

I stepped into her embrace and gave her a hug. She wasn't a hugger usually. "It's good to be home."

"Though keep in mind I'll have his balls if he so much as steps out of line with you again."

"Understood." I smiled. She meant well.

Not much had changed even with the new apartment, and I was glad it felt nice and cozy to be back. All of our stuff had found its home, and even my room was set up much the same.

After unpacking, I logged onto my laptop, ready to look for jobs. I was set on paying Ellie back for the rent. I knew she didn't have much extra money just lying around, and I wanted to pull my fair share. Not to mention I'd go positively crazy without a job. A pang of regret coursed through me at how my job at Status had ended. I certainly wouldn't be getting a recommendation from my former boss. And God, what would I say if someone asked why I'd left my last job? Crap! *My male model boyfriend got my boss pregnant and I quit.* Ha! Yeah right. That'd go over about as well as a fart in church.

I supposed I'd have to spin it . . . say I went home for a family emergency. They didn't need to know the emergency was me having a complete emotional breakdown.

Being in New York and back with Ben was emotionally overwhelming. It would take some time to process. I certainly hadn't expected to run right into his arms again. But then again, nothing about our relationship was expected. I decided last night that I'd give him another chance, and I meant it. But that didn't mean I wasn't going to be warier approaching our relationship this time around. I had both of my eyes wide open, and I would wait to see how it all unfolded. He would need to show me with his actions, and not just pretty words, why he could be trusted again.

2

Ben

My shoot was at an old warehouse in Brooklyn so I was up early and across the Williamsburg Bridge before eight. I wish I could've stayed with Emmy last night, but I didn't want to rush her. I'd done things all wrong the first time around and I was bound and determined to make things better for her. I would go at whatever pace she wanted, take care of her every need, and love her as long as she'd let me. I was one lucky bastard that I'd been forgiven, and it wasn't something I took lightly.

That being said, I knew my limitations. I wasn't good at going slow and didn't trust myself not to try something if she was in the bed next to me. She was too luscious with those tempting curves. And I knew how good she fucked, how soft and silken her skin was, those sexy little noises she made when she came. . . . Damn, I was going to give myself an erection thinking about her like that. And seeing how this was a swimsuit shoot, and I was currently sporting a nut-constricting pair of briefs . . . that wouldn't be good. Not unless I wanted to give everyone on set a show.

Still, I wished I could've spent more time with Emmy. Part of it was that I really didn't like the look of the neighborhood she lived in. I'd already called a local company about installing a security system in their apartment.

Her roommate was a little firecracker, though. I had a feeling that even at 110 pounds tops, she'd give an intruder a swift kick to the balls if needed, a thought that made me feel only marginally better.

Fiona lingered just off set, her eyes roaming my nearly naked form every few moments. I hated how obvious she was and I couldn't believe I'd never noticed it before. Now that Emmy had pointed it out, the way Fiona felt about me was reflected in her eyes, which made it a little difficult to be around her. Annoying, mostly. Nothing I couldn't handle. This was work. Plain and simple.

I pulled my phone from my backpack near the makeup station to send Emmy a quick text before the shoot started. I needed to see her tonight.

Me: Hey baby. I want to take you out for dinner tonight. Are you free?

Emmy: Hiiii! Yes, that'd be great. I've been stuck inside all day looking for jobs.

Me: My driver will pick you up in front of your building at

7:00 and bring you to a restaurant in Midtown. I'll take the train and meet you there.

Emmy: I don't want to hog your car. I'm used to taking the train . . .

Me: No, you'll be safer with Henry (my driver) and I don't want to have to worry about you. See you tonight, baby.

Emmy: See you soon.

As soon as I shoved the phone back into my bag, Fiona approached.

"They're just about ready for you, love. I asked them to adjust the lights so they wouldn't be in your eyes too much."

"Thanks," I muttered.

"You look perfect," she said softly.

I was spray-tanned and my chest and abs were freshly waxed. I'd hit the weight room extra hard the entire month Emmy was gone. I knew I was ready for swim season, which the fashion industry featured during the fall and winter, but I couldn't help but feel the desperation rolling off Fiona in waves. "Should we do it?" I nodded toward the set, rather than acknowledge her compliment.

She led the way, and I trailed behind.

I knew I should tell her about me and Emmy and figured now was a good time. I wouldn't have to see the pain in her eyes. I didn't want to hurt her. "I'm back with Emmy." Best to keep it simple and to the point.

Her head whipped in my direction, her mouth dropping open. "Oh?"

"Yes." So much for not hurting her. Her eyes welled with tears, which she quickly blinked away. She didn't say anything else, just went and sat alone beside the set in a rusty metal folding chair while I got in position for the photographer and tried to act like everything was fine.

Emmy

I wasn't sure where Ben was taking me for dinner but knowing him, it'd be someplace upscale. He didn't strike me as a sandwich-shop kind of guy. It was November in New York, which meant it was colder than Antarctica, or at least Tennessee, which was what my body was used to.

I wasn't sure what to wear so I dressed in leggings with a super-soft cream-colored sweater that was long enough to cover my butt and my tall brown Audrey Boone boots that I'd gotten on sale. I added my navy pea coat then watched the street from our living room window.

Soon a sleek black sedan rolled to a stop at the sidewalk in front of our building. *Henry*. I didn't know anything about this guy but if Ben trusted him, I guessed it was fine.

When I approached the car, he exited and opened the back passenger door for me. I didn't know if I should sit up front since there were just two of us, but I stayed quiet and slid into the backseat.

"Good evening, Miss Clarke," he said.

"Hi. It's Henry, right?"

"Yes ma'am. Ben's asked me to bring you to him at Prime Bistro. I've heard the food is great there."

"Thank you, Henry."

We rode in silence the remainder of the way while soft classical music played in the background. I watched the city come into view from the window, the skyline rising up in front of me, taking my breath away. The high-rises cast glittering reflections on the river while the sun sunk from view in the background. Coupled with the calming music in the otherwise quiet interior, the car was relaxing.

When we arrived at Prime Bistro Henry helped me from the car and I spotted Ben right away, waiting for me just inside the restaurant's entrance.

He was dressed in gray dress pants and a white button-down shirt rolled at the sleeves, a wool jacket resting over his arm. I wondered if he'd worked today and if he'd seen Fiona, but all thoughts of her dissipated when he pulled me snuggly into his arms and pressed a kiss to my mouth.

"Hi, baby." He smiled down at me and all was right with the world.

"Hi," I returned, breathless from his tender and sweet kiss.

Ben took my hand, lacing his fingers between mine, and led me to our waiting table.

The restaurant was small and intimate, with a glowing stone fireplace at its center; creaky wood-plank floors were dotted with linen-covered tables. The aroma of fresh-baked bread and roasted meats permeated the air. A mouthwatering combination, if my reaction was any indication.

"This place is nice," I commented as Ben helped me into an oversized red leather booth in the back.

"It's great. I take my mom here anytime she comes to New York. She and I used to come here when I was a kid." Ben spread his arms across the back of the booth, looking quite comfortable and happy to show me a place from his childhood.

It was nothing like the kid-friendly restaurants my parents had taken me and my brother, Porter, to when we were kids. This wasn't a peanut-shells-on-the-floor-with-a-play-set-in-the-back kind of place. The kind of place with those horribly sticky vinyl plastic tablecloths and grubby plastic menus, where you could be confident kids wouldn't mess up anything. I was often reminded of how different Ben's upbringing was from mine.

When the server appeared, we ordered drinks, a glass of red wine for me and a gin and tonic for him.

"How was your day? Did you work?"

He squeezed the wedge of lime into his drink and took a sip. "Yeah, swimsuit shoot. Went well, but it took longer than expected and I'm starving."

Warm bread was delivered to our table and I buttered a slice for Ben, sliding the saucer toward him. "Here. Eat."

"Food pusher," he murmured under his breath, but one side of his mouth quirked up in a smile.

I buttered a slice for myself next and took a bite. I had to physically suppress my moan, the bread was so good. Crusty on the outside and warm and soft in the center. I hadn't had bread like this since Paris. Ben's eyes lifted and locked on mine. I wondered if he was thinking the same thing. We'd shared so many amazing times together in Paris and I didn't want those memories to be overshadowed by the bitter way things had ended, with Fiona sending me packing in an attempt to keep Ben all to herself.

"What did you do today?" he asked, taking another sip of his drink.

"I looked for jobs all day. Applied to a couple of assistant positions for firms downtown." I'd packed Ellie's lunch before she'd left for work, too, a small sort of peace offering for all my erratic behavior lately. But I knew that'd just earn me another chuckle from him for being a food pusher.

"Any modeling agencies?" he asked, helping himself to a second slice of bread.

I nibbled on the bread in front of me, wondering if that was a twinge of jealousy I'd heard in his voice. He couldn't possibly think that other male models would be interested in me. "No," I confirmed. My adventures in the modeling world were done. I couldn't handle the egos, the cattiness. "Investment banks, advertising agencies, places like that."

He nodded, looking mildly relieved.

The server came by and we placed our order. Grilled salmon for Ben and a chicken Caesar salad for me.

I couldn't help the burning questions still in my head. I wanted to move forward with him, but before I fully could,

I knew I needed more answers. I took a sip of my wine for fortification. "Ben . . ."

"Hmm?"

"Was that the only, uh . . . time that Fiona spent the night with you in Paris?"

He reached across the table and took my hand, his thumb rubbing the back of my knuckles. "Yeah, baby. It was just that one time. She was sobbing and upset, so I couldn't turn her away. I promise you, it wasn't a regular occurrence."

I released a breath I didn't know I was holding. "Okay. It's just that you two were alone in Paris for three weeks without me. And I just feel like I don't know what else might have happened."

He shook his head, bringing my hand to his mouth and pressing a sweet kiss to the back of it. "Don't. Don't do that. I don't want you playing the what-if game, replaying all the possible horrible scenarios in your brain. I was faithful to you, in my heart and in my head. I was too drunk to realize what was happening, and my body got used against me. It's no excuse and I've regretted that night every day since then. It wasn't clear to me at the time, but looking back, I know Fiona's plan had been to seduce me. I never should have opened that door for her. What I woke up to in the middle of the night . . ."

I snatched my hand away. "Ben. Please, not so much detail. It still hurts to think about that night."

"You're right, I'm sorry. I just thought it might help if you knew more about the situation."

I drew a shaky breath. "You're right. It might. But just not right now. I think I'd need more wine for that conversation and I don't want to cry in public, so let's just enjoy our meal."

Fiona had been a constant source of tension in our short relationship so far. I didn't trust her. And I hated that Ben had a weakness where she was concerned. It drove me mad, actually. But accepting him and moving forward with this relationship meant putting up with her. Something I wasn't sure I could do successfully.

The mood between us had changed, grown tense by the time our food was delivered.

"Are you okay?" Ben asked.

I nodded. "I'll be fine."

We ate much of the meal in silence, though his intense gaze often rested on mine. It wasn't my intention to create this silent, tense moment but I wasn't sure how to get back to the easy, flirty banter we used to share.

I wondered if perhaps we weren't meant to have a relationship. Maybe we were nothing more than a fling of convenience, two people living in close quarters who shared a brief, albeit intense, connection.

While Ben paid the check, I excused myself for the ladies room. He met me in the back corridor and escorted me out to the curb. I wasn't sure when he'd called Henry—must have been when I was in the restroom—but his black car was parked along the curb, right in front of the restaurant. This guy was like a ninja, always appearing just in time. It was baffling to me. I'd never known anyone with a car and driver.

Ben turned to face me, cupping my face in his big palms.

"I'm sorry about everything. I'm sorry I ruined dinner. I was trying to take you on a proper date but perhaps it was thoughtless of me. I should have taken you someplace private where we could've talked more."

The sincere look in his deep-set hazel eyes just about undid me. I'd told him I wanted to go on proper dates and then I'd shut down on him in the restaurant, unable to handle the skeletons in his closet that he was willing to be so open about. "No. The date was nice. Thank you for showing me a place that you went to with your mom. That means a lot to me."

He smiled and kissed my lips softly. "You're welcome. I want to share pieces of New York and how I grew up with you." He kissed my forehead. "Come on, let's get in the car and get you out of the cold."

Ben opened the door and I slid across the backseat, allowing him to ease in next to me. Having him close enough that I could smell his cologne was distracting. My body responded instantly to that scent, heart fluttering like a giddy idiot, my palms beginning to sweat.

Ben

I hadn't instructed Henry about where we were going just yet but he pulled into traffic, seeming to understand that I needed a moment to talk to Emmy. Guy code or something.

"What's going on inside that pretty head, baby?" I laced my fingers with hers.

She swallowed a lump in her throat, slowly turning to face me. "It's just . . . maybe we aren't compatible in New York."

Whoa. Where was this coming from? "Of course we are. We know we're compatible physically, emotionally, and intellectually, so why should it matter what city we're in? I'll move us both to Paris tomorrow if you think our relationship works better there."

Her mouth softened, curling into a smile, and I brought her hand to my lips, leaving a damp kiss there.

I couldn't seem to stop touching her. My hand rested against her thigh, clad in black leggings. I wanted to kiss whoever invented these body-hugging things. I bet her ass looked amazing. I wanted to peel them down her legs with my teeth, exposing inch by creamy inch of her skin. "Will you come home with me?"

Her eyes lifted to mine and she blinked in rapid succession, thinking it over. "Just to talk?"

I couldn't lie to her. Not with those pretty grayish-blue eyes locked on mine, looking so sweet and innocent. "We can talk if you want. But I want you to stay the night."

She bit down on her bottom lip, her teeth leaving an impression in the plump flesh. *Shit*. It was getting me hard. "Okay, I can stay over again . . . but I was serious when I said we needed to take our time, date, and go slow."

I trailed my hand higher up her thigh, leaning in close to whisper in her ear. "If you won't let me fuck you, can I at least taste your pussy, baby?"

Emmy let out a tiny whimper and her gaze shot forward to Henry. He wasn't paying us any attention. I paid him enough to forget whatever he'd seen and overheard throughout the years. "He's not listening," I whispered.

"Ben . . ." she groaned, squirming against the leather seat.

I absolutely fucking loved how I could get her hot so easily. I loved watching her response to me. This was way better than texting with her. "We're dating, baby, we're allowed to have some fun, aren't we?" I ran my nose along the curve of her neck, my warm breath causing her skin to respond by breaking out in chill bumps.

She swallowed and gripped the seat beside her.

"Henry, just one stop. My place," I instructed.

Emmy

Ben lived in a historic district in the city with rows of beautifully ornate Victorian homes that had long ago been split into apartments. His was in a quaint redbrick building with a doorman and a red carpet on the sidewalk leading into the foyer. It was very classy and felt safe in an upscale area popular with small families and wealthy bachelors. It suited him perfectly.

We thanked Henry and greeted the night doorman before heading for the elevator.

Once we reached Ben's apartment he tugged me inside, not bothering to turn on the lights. He pressed my back against the wall and lowered his mouth to mine. The moonlight drifting in through the big picture windows and Ben's muscular body pressing into mine caused a moan to escape my throat. He deepened the kiss, his tongue stroking mine so hypnotically. His hips pressed forward, pinning me against the wall, and his hands roamed down my sides, gliding over my hips.

"Fuck, baby, are you trying to kill me with these leggings?"

I didn't know he'd find my leggings sexy, I'd just wanted to be comfortable and cozy.

"See what you do to me?" Ben took my hand and pressed it into his pants-covered erection.

Holy hell. That thing was ready to burst through his zipper. That had to be painful.

"Turn around, let me see your ass." His hands captured my hips and he spun me around.

My cheeks blossomed in heat. I'd forgotten how direct he was, and how hot I found that. He turned me into a horny mess with a single statement. Waiting and going slow was going to be harder than I ever imagined.

He filled his hands with my backside and released a strangled groan. "This ass is mine." He pushed my sweater up out of the way and slowly peeled the leggings down over my bottom and thighs. He pressed a kiss to each cheek then spun me around to face him.

Still planted on his knees, Ben looked up at me, his eyes dark with desire. "Can I taste you, baby?"

I nodded, silently.

He pressed damp kisses along my inner thigh, his breath tickling me and making me squirm. His hands captured my hips so he could hold me in place while he slowly tortured me. Soft, tender lips tenderly caressed my thighs as he moved closer to my center. No way was I fighting this. I could already feel myself getting wet and he'd hardly touched me. Removing his hands from my hips, Ben pulled my panties down my legs, leaving them at my calves. I was still wearing my boots so this would have to do. He pressed forward, lightly kissing the top of my pubic bone.

Seeing Ben on his knees before me, worshipping my lady parts, was the most glorious sight in the world. I planted a hand in his dark hair and let out a breathy cry. "Bennn . . ."

His mouth covered me, greedily licking my folds, finding my clit and stroking it again and again in a brutal rhythm.

Holy crap!

My knees buckled and I nearly collapsed, but Ben caught me before I ended up in a tangled heap on the floor. Good thing, too, because I was sure to look like a moron with my panties and leggings shoved around my ankles. He lifted me into his arms and carried me to his bed, depositing me safely on the edge. He helped me remove my boots, pulling them off one by one and letting them drop to the floor with a thud.

I knew I'd told him we needed to slow our physical relationship—and I'd meant it—but in this moment slowing down was the last thing I wanted.

I helped him remove my clothing, kicking my panties from my legs in the most unladylike fashion.

Ben chuckled softly. It was obvious how needy I was for his touch. "Take this off, baby."

I raised my arms to allow him to pull the sweater over my head.

Once he'd stripped me naked, he resumed kissing my

thighs, working his way toward my center, but my hand on his shoulder stopped his progression.

"Ben . . . your clothes, too . . . off," I murmured, disoriented.

"Baby, if I get naked with you, I don't know how far things might go and I don't want to push you."

I didn't care about him having restraint just then. The idea of having to use condoms didn't stab at my heart the way it had the other day. "Take them off."

Ben stood next to the bed, quickly shedding his clothes into a pile on the floor.

Standing in front of me, so tall and strong, Ben's body provided an amazing view. His manhood was heavy and long and standing at attention for me. I reached out, wrapping my hand around him. His cock was so warm against my palm and I stroked him slowly from base to tip, loving the solid feel of him. He was so thick that my fingers didn't completely close around him.

A shuddering breath hitched in his throat. "Shit, baby, watching your little hand trying to jerk me off is the hottest thing ever."

I added a second hand, pumping him firmly. I wanted to make him feel good, to be consumed with desire for me.

He groaned when my hands moved together over his sensitive head. "Ah, fuck baby." His entire body tightened, his abdominal muscles contracting deliciously. His hand caught mine. "You gotta stop. You're going to make me come."

I looked up at him in wonder. He was truly so beautiful. "You don't want to?"

"Not tonight. We're going slow, remember?"

I nodded obediently. Me and my dumb rules. "But won't you be, um, uncomfortable later?"

"Don't worry about it. I'll take care of it later. All I want to do is get you off. That's it." He leaned down and kissed my mouth. "No sex. And you don't even have to touch me."

I pouted, my bottom lip jutting out. "But what if I want to?" I whimpered. I reached for his thick erection again but Ben's hand caught my wrist.

"No. This time's all about you." Ben gently shoved my shoulders back and I fell against the bed.

I was still soaking wet from his earlier attention, and Ben wasted no time rubbing my slickened sex. His index finger made slow, sweeping circles around my folds.

I whimpered when his finger finally made contact with my clit.

"That feel good, honey?" He pressed a kiss to the inside of my thigh. "Tell me, baby. Tell me this is what you want."

"Yes, Ben, that feels good," I panted, reaching for his length. "But I want you . . ."

He slid a finger inside me. "Not tonight. We're waiting, remember?" His cocky grin begged me to disagree.

I moaned, both from frustration and pleasure.

Ben sunk to the bed, bringing his mouth in line with my navel, and slowly dragged his tongue down. I lifted my hips in the hopes of getting more contact with the glorious friction of his tongue. But he moved slowly, unrushed, gently kissing and nibbling my tummy.

Finally he settled where I needed him and kissed me tenderly, his warm mouth covering me. Within just moments of his skillful tongue sliding against me, I was done, finished, completely and utterly devastated. I came apart, loudly moaning his name.

Afterward, Ben tucked me in against his side, cocooning his body around mine, and held me while the aftershocks of my release pulsed through my body. I couldn't help but notice he was still rock-hard, but he didn't complain. He seemed to have just what he wanted: me in his bed, wrapped up tightly in his arms.

3

Ben

I let Emmy sleep in while I prepared coffee, toasted bagels, and sliced some fruit. Perfectly timed, my beautiful girl came strolling out of the bedroom thirty minutes later. Just the sight of her, sleepy and walking toward me barefoot across my space, made my heart pump faster. She meant everything to me and I'd never risk losing her again.

Her hair was mussed, tangled, and sticking up in odd directions and she was dressed in a pair of my boxer briefs, which hung off her hips in a really sexy way, and an old tank top of mine I used for working out. She looked so fuckable. I wanted to tear the boxers down her legs and take her on the kitchen counter.

Fuck.

"Morning." My voice came out strangled. I cleared my throat and tried again. "Hi."

"Hi," she returned, her voice whisper soft.

"Would you like some coffee?"

She nodded.

I poured her a mug of coffee and Emmy grabbed some plates for our breakfast. I liked being side by side with her in my kitchen. It felt very natural. I had my other half back.

"Do you have plans tonight?" I asked.

She shook her head. "I was just planning on looking for more jobs to apply to."

"I was wondering if you'd come to an industry thing with me tonight."

"An industry thing?"

"Yeah, it's like a cocktail mixer for designers, photographers, and models. I should probably go for a little bit and I was hoping you'd be free to come with me."

Emmy placed some sliced berries on her plate, keeping her eyes down. "Will Fiona be there?"

"Yeah, I think so."

"Oh." She dropped her chin to her chest.

"Hey." I set the carton of milk on the counter and stepped closer, tipping her chin up to meet my eyes. "We're not going to hide what we have from her. We have no reason to tiptoe around her."

She inhaled deeply. "You're right. It'll just be hard. I haven't seen her since . . . you know, everything went down. . . ."

"I know. But I'll be right by your side the whole night. Braydon will be there, too. We could even invite Ellie, make a night of it. It could be fun."

She nodded, a little smile curling her mouth. "Yeah, okay.

I'll ask Ellie about it. We usually don't do much besides catch up on TV shows on Sunday night anyways."

"Come here." I opened my arms and Emmy willingly walked into them. Pulling her against my chest, I hated the way her mouth had pressed into a firm line at the mention of Fiona's name. I wanted to take away all her painful memories and make new ones that made her smile. "You sleep okay?" I wanted to get back to a lighter mood between us. Things had been too tense lately.

She nodded, wrapping her arms around my waist. It was no coincidence that I'd left my shirt off. I wasn't going to pressure her into sex, but hell, I was still a guy and the idea of tempting her a bit was just too much to pass up. Her little hands skittered up my sides over my ribs. Then her fingers dug in and twisted, tickling me.

"Ah! Hey now . . ." I stepped back out of her reach. The little brat.

She laughed softly. "I wanted to see if you were ticklish."

"Yeah?" I stepped in closer, narrowing my eyes. "You sure you want to get into a tickle war with me?" I cracked my knuckles. "Because I can be ruthless, baby."

Emmy lifted an arched brow and took a step back. "You wouldn't."

"Oh I would." I stepped closer to her then stopped myself. "I'll give you a head start." My eyes flicked to the bedroom then back to her, mischievously. Emmy took off running. Her ass looked so fucking cute, filling out the boxers in a way I never would.

Sprinting to the bedroom, I found her perched on the bed resting on her knees, pillow in hand like she was ready for battle. I liked seeing her playful side. As soon as I got close enough, *whump*, she hit me square in the chest with the pillow.

"Uh-oh, someone's being a naughty girl." I reached out to remove the weapon from her hand. "Let's just place this over here." I dropped the pillow to the floor beside the bed and climbed toward her like a cheetah stalking a gazelle. A sexy fucking gazelle. That I wanted to nail. Badly.

Her teeth sunk into her bottom lip again and she watched me approach.

In a single quick maneuver, I had her on her back. I pinned her wrists above her head, my body holding hers hostage with my weight on top of her.

Emmy, now restrained against the bed, only had the use of her legs. She wrapped those around my hips, tugging against me. "You think that's going to help you get away?" I whispered.

She pulled in a shuddering breath, growing quiet. Her eyes were huge, watching mine, waiting to see what I'd do.

The feel of her body struggling against mine, her soft breath tickling my neck, her hips bucking underneath me . . . *shit*. I was hard. And the thin athletic shorts provided very little in the way of a barrier. Her body froze midstruggle as awareness hit her. The entire mood of our playful wrestling match changed in an instant.

My erection nudged at her center.

Emmy whimpered.

Fuck, so this little thing liked being restrained. That information was not helping. I needed to keep my mind out of the damn gutter.

Emmy pressed her hips up, grinding against my dick. Fuck, that felt good. I needed to explain to him that he couldn't go in there. In that warm, tight channel . . . yeah, thinking about it was so not helping. I held my breath, waiting for the sensation to pass. I counted backward from ten. I thought about sports, math equations, world hunger . . . yeah, nothing was going to help this monster of an erection. I wanted her. Bad.

I imagined ripping off her shorts then pushing down my own and sinking into her. Right here, right now. I'd fuck her slowly, holding her wrists in my hands. I'd fuck her until she was moaning out my name. My cock twitched in my shorts. *Shit*. It was either fuck her senseless or walk away. I couldn't take this torture.

"I'm going to, um, shower. Then I'll drive you home."

She nodded, wordlessly, her breath coming in little gasps.

And I was going to jerk off in the shower, too, but she didn't need to know that part.

4

Emmy

When the car was just around the corner, Ben sent me a warning text that he was almost here. I called out to Ellie, who was still in her room getting ready.

"I just need two minutes!" she called back.

I shoved my feet into the beautiful black Christian Louboutin platform heels that Ben had given to me in Paris. I loved these shoes. I felt sexy anytime I was wearing them. My deep purple dress was modest, falling to the knee with a bisecting cut on top that showed just a small peek of cleavage.

I looked out the window and saw a long black stretch limo rolling to a stop at the curb in front of the building. "They're here, Ellie." I added my long, black trench coat, shrugging it on over my dress. There was no getting around the fact that winter was almost here, and I'd choose warmth over sexiness every time. Hopefully the event had a coat check.

"I'm ready." Ellie sauntered from her bedroom in a pretty dark-gray dress that looked soft and black suede wedges. Her hair was twisted up in a sleek bun and she'd ditched the glasses for contacts. Her lips were stained a dark berry color. She looked incredible.

"Wow. You look great."

She shrugged into her coat. "Thanks. You look stunning." Her eyes roamed my ensemble.

Once we reached the curb, Ben climbed out and held open the door. His heated gaze caressed my curves. "Hi, baby," he whispered, low enough for only me to hear. He looked so handsome in his black tailored suit, white shirt, and dark-gray tie.

Ellie climbed inside the limo and I scooted in next to her.

"Bray!" I hadn't known that he'd be riding with Ben. I thought we'd meet him there.

"Hi, jellybean." Braydon smiled at me warmly. "You look good enough to eat."

Ben settled in beside me and narrowed his eyes, shooting Bray a death glare. I knew Ben didn't like thinking about me with Braydon any more than I liked thinking about him with Fiona.

"Oh boy, this douche canoe again. . . ." Ellie muttered under her breath.

I bit my cheek to keep from smiling. She often made up her own words to describe things and apparently the sight of Braydon inspired his own neologism. Impressive considering we hadn't even had a drink yet.

"Yesss . . . the firecracker! Elizabeth, right?" Braydon grinned widely.

"Ellie," she reminded him.

Ben handed me and Ellie glasses of champagne. He and Braydon had already mixed some cocktails.

It felt a little strange to be sharing a limo with Ben and Braydon, knowing what had happened the last time the three of us were together, but I tried to push it from my mind.

"Remind me, how do you two know each other?" Ellie asked, glancing in my direction.

"I met Braydon in Paris. He's a friend of Ben's." *That's my story and I'm sticking to it.*

She pursed her lips and nodded. Ben wasn't exactly her favorite topic right now. I knew she was afraid of me getting hurt.

"So what do you do for a living?" Ellie asked Braydon.

I thought she knew Bray was a model, or maybe she was just trying to make polite conversation.

"Gynecologist," he answered with a completely straight face. "You?"

"Proctologist," Ellie returned, meeting his gaze without so much as blinking.

"Sweet. If I ever need my ass looked at, I know who to call."

She frowned. "I'm not taking on new clients."

"That's a damn shame. If you need me to examine you, just let me know. I'm extremely gentle. Vaginas love me and I always ensure a happy ending."

Ellie rolled her eyes, scoffing loudly, while I giggled into my hand.

Ben and I watched their back-and-forth like a game of Ping-Pong. Wow. These two were all intense stares and biting tones. I wasn't sure if it was a dry-sarcastic way of flirting or if Ellie truly wasn't a fan. But they were rather amusing to watch. Ben and I stayed glued to their heated exchange throughout the ride.

When we reached the art gallery my nerves went haywire. I didn't know how I'd handle seeing Fiona live and in person. I hoped I didn't flip out. Ben helped me from the car, resting his hand on my lower back as he guided me to the entrance.

Once Ellie and I had checked our coats and I tucked the coat-check ticket into my purse, we followed Ben and Bray to the bar to grab a drink. A drink was exactly what I needed in my trembling hands.

The art gallery was a small, intimate gathering. About fifty people mingled, talking and drinking in a narrow room hung with bright colorful paintings on the otherwise white walls.

I clutched the stem of the glass of champagne so hard I thought it might snap off in my hand. I was wound impossibly tight at the prospect of spotting Fiona, laughing and mingling in the crowd. If she approached Ben and tried to air-kiss his cheeks or clutch onto his bicep like she used to, I might lose it. I wondered if it was a felony to attack a pregnant woman. Perhaps if I just explained to the police officer what a mega-bitch she was, any and all crimes would be pardoned.

Ben, reading my tense posture, guided our group over to a less crowded corner of the gallery.

"Emmy? You okay, sweetie?" Ellie gave me a concerned look.

"I don't know what I'm going to do if I have to face Fiona," I admitted. Ben caught my eyes and frowned but stayed quiet.

Ellie raised her hand, catching the attention of the waiter circulating with a silver tray of champagne glasses and waved him over to us. "You got anything stronger back at the bar?" she asked.

He nodded. "I think so."

She pulled a crisp fifty-dollar bill from her wristlet. "Here's your tip. Keep them coming."

The waiter arrived with two Jack and Cokes. Ellie handed me both. "Thanks."

I focused on sucking down the refreshing cocktail through the little straw and let my eyes wander the room. I was grateful at least to be surrounded by Ben, Braydon, and Ellie, who all seemed to be understanding.

After I'd finished my first cocktail, I saw someone trying to catch Ben's attention. "Will you be okay for a bit? There's a few people I need to go talk to," Ben said.

"Of course. I'll stay with Ellie." I knew he was here for work, and I didn't want my insecurities to keep him from doing his job and making the connections he needed.

I watched Ben mingle with a group of men on the far side of the room. I didn't know who they were but they looked like arty types—photographers, designers, and such. Feeling a little more confident, my gaze wandered. The moment I spotted her, it was like all the air was sucked from the room. I hadn't been prepared that she'd actually look pregnant, or that she'd have the cutest baby bump ever. My knees locked together and I struggled to remain standing. I pulled in a deep, shaky breath.

Fiona was glowing, her skin was radiant, and her bright, white smile gleamed as she chatted casually with the man beside her. She was dressed in a pretty black dress, her little belly protruding in a barely there round bump, and soft waves of perfectly styled hair flowed over her shoulders. A pair of leopard-print ballet flats completed the look. She'd apparently given up her sky-high heels she normally wore for something more modest.

"You okay?" Ben approached me from behind, pulling my attention away from Fiona. His hand came to a rest against my spine, like he knew I'd need the physical support.

I swallowed a mouthful of bitter saliva. "Another drink. Get me another drink," I bit out.

He signaled the poor waiter, who was earning every last bit of that tip, and moments later I had a fresh Jack and Coke in my hand. I sucked it down greedily.

Fiona's hand rested against her belly as she circulated the room and chatted with various industry people. Her eyes had wandered to Ben and me once, and he'd placed his arm protectively around my waist, pulling me closer. Fiona had kept going right on past us. I was glad I didn't have to speak to her but even seeing her made me sick.

Several drinks later, I was clutching Ben's arm just to keep vertical. He tipped my chin up to meet his eyes. His worried gaze locked on mine and I could see him mentally calculating how many drinks I'd had. "You ready for me to take you home, baby?"

I nodded, drunkenly. "Yeah. I'm just going to go to the bathroom."

Ben motioned for Ellie to take me, and after linking her arm through mine we headed through the gallery, thankfully without spotting Fiona on the way.

Ellie and I each slipped inside a stall and went about our business. But when I emerged, Fiona was standing at the sink inspecting her makeup.

Shit.

I took a deep breath and calmly approached the sink next to her and began soaping my hands. Maybe all that alcohol wasn't the best idea. My stomach was churning violently and I felt woozy and disoriented under the harsh fluorescent lighting. I watched in silence as Fiona reapplied berry-red lipstick to her perfect pout.

I rinsed the suds from my hands and found my reflection in the mirror. In contrast to Fiona's perfectly put-together appearance I was pale and . . . drunk looking.

Just great.

"It's a nice event, isn't it?" I attempted politeness, breaking the stony silence between us.

She shrugged, recapping her tube of lipstick and dropping it inside her tiny purse. "I am surprised to see you here, actually. Ben hadn't said anything about you two being back together."

Her words stung, I couldn't lie. Ben should have told her to go to hell and that I was the love of his life. Why hadn't he? While I was still rendered speechless, Fiona turned to face me. *God, where the hell was Ellie?*

"Enjoy him now while you can." Her hand lovingly caressed her belly. "We're going to be a family soon. We'll have a forever connection. What will you have? Your memories of a great shag?"

I swallowed the dry lump in my throat, fighting back the tears and curse words I wanted to let rip. I opened my mouth, my intoxicated brain struggling to give voice to the words swirling in my brain.

"He's stuck by me for five years. Don't forget that sweetie. I'd be careful if I were you," she warned, bitter venom lacing her voice.

Ellie emerged from the stall just then, standing tall beside me. "What Emmy and Ben have is none of your damn business, you old witch. Just worry about yourself." Ellie's tone was careful, measured, and I was thankful for her clear, level head. But her voice held a hint of warning, too, and I knew she could go from civilized to bitch in two seconds flat.

Fiona looked from Ellie back to me and let out a short laugh. "Enjoy yourselves while it lasts, girls." She placed the little purse strap over her wrist and strolled from the restroom without a backward glance.

I learned that being highly intoxicated and emotionally

drained from my showdown with Fiona didn't mix well. When we found the guys again, Ben's mouth tugged down in a frown and he looped an arm around my waist. "Come on, let's get you home."

I merely nodded and let him guide me to the exit, hoping that Fiona was somewhere nearby watching his arms encircle me.

The hiccups hit me on the limo ride back. Ben watched me with a worried expression and Ellie handed me a bottle of water from the limo minibar while Braydon sat slumped in the seat next to Ben.

"Here, sweetie, drink this." She uncapped the bottle and urged me to take a sip.

The water should have been refreshing, but my belly was turning somersaults and my head was spinning from facing the wrong direction in the limo. I took a small sip and returned the bottle. I let my eyes slip close and rested my head back against the leather headrest.

The three of them continued a low, murmured conversation beside me, and I tried to focus on what was being said since I was pretty sure they were discussing me.

"Your agent is a fucking bitch," Ellie snapped.

"She means well, Ellie, trust me. You don't know her like I do."

"Yeah, right. She meant well when she was in the restroom just now telling Emmy that she was going to win you back."

Braydon cleared his throat loudly but Ben remained

quiet. I wanted him to argue, to shout and curse and swear that it was never going to happen. But his silence permeated the air, making my stomach turn in little somersaults.

"You think this is healthy for her? Being with you? Having to deal with this shit?" Ellie whispered coarsely.

"I don't know," Ben answered.

I wanted to argue with them, to tell them I was fine. Or that I would be once this damn limo stopped spinning. It was like a magic-carpet ride from hell. But I stayed quiet, trying to piece together their cryptic, murmured phrases.

Ben cursed under his breath. "I'm not giving her up. As long as she wants me, I'm here."

I vaguely heard Ben instruct the driver to bring us home first then drop off Ellie and Braydon after. I hoped they would be okay alone together. For some reason they mixed about as well as oil and water. But I didn't have time to worry about that. My attention was focused solely on praying that the contents of my stomach would stay put. By the time the limo rolled to a stop in front of Ben's building, I'd lost the use of my legs. *Well, shit.*

Ben lifted me in his arms and carried me. When we reached his apartment, he brought me inside and set me down on the couch then removed my shoes. "Are you feeling okay?"

I nodded, though I wasn't entirely sure. *God, why did I drink so much?*

"I'll go get you a glass of water and some pain reliever," he said.

His words barely registered because the second he was out of the living room I was on my feet, darting for the bathroom. The liquor in my stomach churned violently and just as the toilet came into view I lost it, sinking to my knees and getting sick.

Ew. I hated throwing up. The coughing, the smell, the violent way my stomach kept convulsing long after I'd emptied it.

After I had thoroughly expelled everything from my system, I collapsed onto the floor in a heap. It was only then that I noticed Ben was beside me. *Shit.* He pushed the hair back from my face. I tried to focus on his perfect face but he was too blurry. The bathroom was tipping and spinning rather annoyingly. I was vaguely aware of his arms coming around me and lifting me off the floor before the world went black.

Ben

Emmy was dead weight in my arms. I hated seeing her like this, knowing she felt like shit. I placed her on my bed and went about removing her dress, bra, and panties. I dressed her in a pair of my boxer shorts and a T-shirt. My lucky Yankees shirt. Maybe it would make her feel better.

She curled into a ball in the center of my bed. "Benn . . ." Her arm flailed out, her hand searching for me in a grabby motion.

"I'm right here, baby." I gripped her hand, sliding my fingers between hers. "Shh. I've got you."

"My head hurts," she croaked.

"Let's get you settled." I shifted her so that she was positioned higher up on the mattress and slid a pillow underneath her head, then I pulled the comforter around her. "How's that?"

She didn't answer right away, and I was wondering if she'd passed out.

"You saw me barf."

I suppressed a chuckle. "You were sick, honey. I wanted to take care of you."

"I'm s-sorry. . . ." she groaned.

"It's okay, pretty girl. Just rest, okay?" I smoothed the hair back from her face. She looked so sweet, so vulnerable, passed out drunk against my pillow, dressed in my Yankees T-shirt. I continued just watching her, caressing her cheek and tucking her hair behind her ear.

She mumbled something unintelligible. "Bennn . . ." she groaned.

Shit. I was about to lift her up and carry her back to the bathroom just in case she was going to be sick again. "Yeah, baby?"

Emmy pouted, her bottom lip jutting out like she might cry. "She looked really pretty . . . she had a cute tummy. . . ."

What?

Oh.

Pregnant Fiona.

Emmy's brow crinkled in concentration as she fought sleep. "She's having a . . . a b-baby, and it might be your baby, right, Ben?"

"I don't think it's my baby." I choked on the words. We were seriously discussing this *now*? I almost considered leaving her to sleep but I was too curious to hear what else she might say.

"Me and you are gonna make pretty babies," she said.

Holy shit. Was she serious? I didn't want a baby.

"The prettiest," I agreed. "Now sleep, honey." I patted her butt and she let out a soft groan.

Fuck. I paced the living room floor. I couldn't handle seeing Emmy like this . . . and then hearing her talk about wanting a baby . . . with me? Maybe it was just the alcohol talking, but shit. I was nowhere near ready for a baby. I was still learning about how to be a boyfriend. And I wasn't even very good at that.

Too keyed up for sleep, I sat down on the armchair with my iPad.

5

Emmy

The room was much too bright, and my throat felt raw and scratchy. I blinked my eyes open and attempted to swallow.

Ouch.

It was raw and irritated.

What the hell happened last night?

Oh God. Memories flashed into focus. Fiona with her perfect little baby bump. Me binging on liquor. I struggled to remember what happened after that.

I blinked at my surroundings. Ben lay next to me, asleep and resting peacefully, his hair rumpled from sleep and a crease across one cheek.

I was glad I was here with him but how had I gotten into his bed?

Memories of getting sick in his bathroom and him tucking me into bed danced in my subconscious.

God, my head was pounding.

I flung off the blankets and climbed from the bed on unsteady legs, trying to be as quiet as possible. I wanted to let him sleep. I shuffled to the kitchen for a glass of water. I'd downed half of it when my stomach grumbled loudly. Rather than finishing the water, like my parched throat craved, I heeded the advice of my stomach and set the glass of water on the counter. We'd need to take it easy today.

I heated up the shower to wash last night's makeup and grime from my skin. The water felt divine, and after shampooing my hair with Ben's all-purpose hair-and-body wash that smelled like light, crisp cologne, I wrapped myself in a fluffy towel and shuffled back to the bedroom. I redressed in the pajamas he must have put me in—boxers and a T-shirt.

When I climbed in beside him Ben rolled toward me and covered my body in a hug. "Mmm, morning baby. . . ." he mumbled, his lips brushing my collarbone.

"Morning." I curled into him, tangling my legs with his.

"How are you feeling?"

"Okay. A little queasy," I admitted.

"I can make you some toast if you like."

"That's all right. I should probably get home." Nothing like overstaying your welcome. He was used to having his own space, peace, and quiet, I was sure.

His arms tightened around me. "You're not going anywhere today."

I laughed softly. "Oh, really?"

"You're mine today. Know that."

I smiled at his conviction. I loved knowing I was his. Hopefully I didn't do anything too awkward when I was drunk last night. "Thanks for taking care of me."

"Of course, baby. You were kind of cute."

My brows squeezed together, struggling to remember what I might have done or said. "Did I, um, say anything embarrassing last night?"

His body stiffened over the top of mine. "Don't worry about that. You were drunk." He climbed from the bed, tossing a T-shirt over his head and leaving me to wonder what I'd possibly said that had him acting standoffish.

Shit.

"Ben?"

He looked down at the plush carpeting. "You, ah, mentioned something about us having pretty babies."

"Oh." Well, that was dumb. Sheesh, why couldn't I have kept my mouth shut? Alcohol was like truth serum for me. Things I didn't mean to say just spewed out, apparently. "I'm sorry about that," I apologized weakly.

He shook his head. "I'll make you something to eat."

"Okay." It wasn't lost on me that he didn't address my baby comment. He'd all but fled the room. *Dammit.*

I ventured into the bathroom, combed my hair, and secured it in a braid over my shoulder. I knew I was stalling but I just needed a minute before facing him. We hadn't even been dating long, and now I was talking about having a baby with him. Lord, help me. I wouldn't blame him if he went running for the hills. Several moments later I joined him in the kitchen.

He had brewed coffee and was rummaging through his nearly empty fridge. "That mug's for you, babe. I'm trying to see what I can make you."

I wrapped my hands around the warm coffee cup and peeked around Ben's shoulder. The fridge contained an odd collection of condiments and expensive bottled water.

"Looks like I'll have to go out hunting and gathering to feed my woman." Ben smiled warmly, pressing a tender kiss to my forehead. "Anything in particular sound good?"

I shook my head. Tolerating any food with my shaky stomach would be a miracle.

"I've got just the thing: Benji's House of Noodles. Hang-over-cure food. Trust me. I'll be back in a little bit."

"That's sweet of you to offer, but maybe I should just head home. I won't make very good company today. I'm hungover, PMSing . . ." I paused. *Oops*. Hadn't really meant to say that part out loud.

Ben raised an eyebrow. "Hush. I'm taking care of you today. It won't take me long to grab the food."

His palate was surely more adventurous than mine. He was well traveled, and had lived in New York City for many years, one of the most culturally diverse places in the world. I didn't think my queasy stomach could handle curry or any-thing too spicy or adventurous right now. But I merely nod-ded. I trusted him. I just didn't trust my stomach.

"Go relax." He gave me a gentle pat on the butt. "Advil's in the bathroom cabinet. I'll be back soon."

I crawled into bed when Ben left, and though I hadn't expected to fall asleep, the sound of the front door closing woke me a little while later.

I ventured into the kitchen and found Ben unpacking cartons of food on the butcher-block island in the kitchen. Fragrant aromas of garlic and sautéed chicken and vegetables greeted me. It smelled terrific and my stomach grumbled at the thought of something warm to fill it.

Ben gathered bowls from the cabinet and dumped the contents of the containers inside. "You'll love this place. It's a favorite of mine when I'm in New York. Just don't tell Fiona." His gaze flicked to mine, his eyes wide, like he couldn't believe he'd just spoken her name.

I involuntarily flinched, but quickly recovered, shrugging it off. "My lips are sealed." I smiled.

Ben's easy smile returned as he recovered from his faux pas of mentioning she who must not be named.

The sight of the thin noodles tossed in light sauce with chicken and julienned vegetables made my mouth water. It wasn't a conventional breakfast but considering it was already noon, it was perfect.

Ben poured us each a glass of ice water from a filtered pitcher in the fridge and we took our bowls of noodles into the living room. Settling on the couch, I took a big bite. Ben watched me, waiting for my reaction.

"Awesome, isn't it?"

"Oh my God," I moaned through the mouthful of noodles. "Don't talk to me." I held up a hand, chewing slowly to savor the flavors. "Good Lord, that's good," I confirmed, digging in for another bite.

Ben chuckled and took a bite of his own. "Told you. I swear they put crack in their food. It's fucking addictive."

I nodded, happily stuffing another bite of the delicious noodles into my mouth. Once my entire bowl was gone, I stopped myself from actually licking the sauce from the bottom of the dish and instead let Ben put it in the dishwasher. Lounging back against the sofa, I rubbed my full belly. Gosh, this thing could almost rival Fiona's right now. My little food bump.

I decided to text Ellie to let her know I was staying at Ben's.

Me: Bad PMS. And a hangover. He's pampering me so gonna stay here. :)

Ellie: Lucky girl. Guys I've dated usually want anal sex when I'm on my period. He's a keeper! Lol.

I chuckled and stuffed my phone back into my purse. Lord, that girl cracked me up.

"Everything okay?" Ben asked, an amused expression on his face.

I realized I'd just been caught laughing to myself. "Fine." I didn't want to tell him about Ellie's *anal* comment. No sense giving him ideas. But she was right, he was a keeper.

6

Emmy

Dating in New York was fun, exotic, and exhausting. We'd been to the Metropolitan Museum of Art, dined at authentic ethnic restaurants in Chinatown and Little Italy, visited Broadway and the American Ballet Theatre, and spent an entire chilly Saturday at the Central Park Zoo, where Ben had been once before as a child and of course I'd never seen.

We shared cocktails at cozy bars, and Ben taught me the fine art of slurping freshly shucked oysters at a quaint riverside seafood bar. He knew New York City and he'd taken dating and going slow to the next level. I'd never been so thoroughly wined and dined. And yet so sexually frustrated.

I was ready to take things to the next level but each night after our dates he'd either drop me off at home with Ellie or tuck me into his bed with a sweet kiss on the nights I stayed there. Nothing more.

Deciding to take matters into my own hands, I'd planned our date for that Saturday night. After consulting Ellie on what type of date might get Ben's blood flowing in the right direction, and declining her idea of visiting a strip club together, I settled on taking him for dessert. Chocolate fondue, specifically.

I'd planned this romantic date and tonight was supposed to be all about me and him, but after spending my entire Saturday searching online and applying for jobs, I was frustrated and tired. I felt down about myself. For all the work I'd put in so far, I'd gotten only two calls in response to my résumé. And neither looked promising.

I was in the middle of apologizing to Ellie about my lack of ability to pay half the rent when Ben arrived.

His knock on the door interrupted a tense moment and I answered, giving him a quick peck on the cheek.

"You look gorgeous, babe." His hand settled against my hip. "Are you ready?"

"I'm sorry, but can you just give us a minute? I was discussing something with Ellie."

"Of course." He patted my behind as he'd grown fond of doing.

Ellie shook her head. "Will you please take your girl out tonight, get her drunk, and tell her to stop worrying? Give her the dick or something because she needs some serious stress relief."

"Ellie," I warned.

"And since I hear you're hung like a hippo, I'm guessing that large love-stick would do the trick."

Crossing the room, I slapped a hand over Ellie's mouth then shot a worried glance at Ben. His expression was amused, and not the least bit embarrassed.

"She said that, huh? A hippo?" A slow smile twitched across his mouth as his lips slowly curved upward. He was gorgeous when he smiled.

Giving him a look of apology, I bit my cheek.

Ben's answering grin told me he wasn't the least bit shy that I'd shared this information. "I'll see what I can do to de-stress her, but first tell me what all this is about." He shoved his hands in his pockets and waited.

Ellie removed my hand from her mouth. "Emmy's freaking out because she hasn't found a job yet. I told her not to worry about the rent. I picked up some overtime and I have it covered."

Ben's easy smile disappeared, curving into a frown. I'd been avoiding bringing him into my drama. I knew I'd find a job eventually, I just didn't know why it was taking so long. "How much is her rent here? I'll take care of it," he said, his tone stern and unyielding.

"No. Ben, you're not paying my rent." I knew he had money but this was ridiculous.

He waved me off, still looking directly at Ellie, waiting for her response.

"Her half is nine hundred," she squeaked out.

Traitor. Damn her. He was intimidating when he pinned you with that stare. I knew that from experience. It seemed Ellie wasn't immune to it, either.

I faced him, planting my hands on my hips. "Ben, don't worry about it. I'm going to find a job." I would. Soon. Even if I had to work at the coffee shop up the street. I'd figure it out.

His gaze slid down my body, caressing my curves. "Emmy."

The careful way my name rolled off his tongue and the soft warning in his tone sent a tingle of awareness zipping down my spine. I found it difficult to disobey him in any fashion. I was needy for him, for his approval, and I subconsciously wanted to please him. In all things. My hands dropped from my hips in silent obedience. I'd missed him so much during our time apart. It had changed something in me.

"There's something I want to talk to you about," he said.

"Okay. Now?"

"No. Let's wait until we get there and grab a drink."

My stomach did a little flip-flop. I hoped it wasn't anything bad. But why else would he want me sitting down with a drink in hand? "Okay." I grabbed my purse and coat and let him lead me outside.

Henry drove us to the café I'd selected and dropped us off right in front, which was good because it was freezing out.

Soon Ben and I were seated in a cozy leather booth in the back corner of a dimly lit wine and dessert café. Giant snowflakes—the first of the season—were falling against a darkened sky outside. It was pretty, magical, and romantic.

I shrugged off my pea coat and Ben hung it on the hooks by our table. I was dressed in black ankle pants and a burgundy silk blouse with a chunky gold necklace. Ben looked yummy, as always. His dress shirt was unbuttoned at the neck, rolled at the sleeves, and only one half of the front was tucked in—showing off his belt and the bulge in the front of his jeans, which was rather impressive. *Focus, Emmy!* Tonight was about showing him I was ready for more.

We sat with glasses of ruby-colored wine, sipping them and chatting as I wondered what he wanted to talk to me about. We made small talk about his latest shoot—there was a live tiger there. It was for some luxury men's brand I'd never heard of, but apparently using a tiger was the ultimate display of masculinity.

When our chocolate fondue arrived we both leaned forward to inspect the goods: a couple of long, two-tined forks, bite-sized pieces of angel food cake, luscious ripe red strawberries, sliced bananas, and brownies cut into quarters. *Mmmm.* Ben grabbed a slice of banana while I went for a strawberry.

The first bite exploded on my taste buds. Warm silken chocolate danced on my tongue and sweet droplets of juice from the berry mixed in an enticing way. This was the perfect meal, in my opinion. Taking a sip of the red wine, I let the flavors mingle.

When I opened my eyes Ben was still watching me, his dark gaze penetrating and possessive. It sent a pulse of heat racing through my core.

He picked up a piece of the brownie next, setting it on his plate. "Good choice, this place."

"Thanks." I beamed at the small compliment, happy that I could bring Ben somewhere he had never been. . . . After swallowing another sip of my wine for courage I asked, "What did you want to talk to me about?"

Ben didn't hesitate. "I just got booked for a job in Fiji. I want you to come."

His tone left little room for negotiation. I knew I should've pointed out that I needed to be here, looking for jobs, hopefully attending interviews, but that wasn't what my brain immediately jumped to. "Will Fiona be there with you?" I didn't want them left unattended again.

He nodded, his gaze darting down to his plate. He picked up the piece of brownie, swirled it in the melted chocolate sauce, then held it before my lips. "Open," he whispered.

I obeyed and Ben fed me a bite of the decadent dessert. Something about the way he watched me while I chewed had all my nerve endings firing. Could I really go with him to Fiji? Could I handle an extended stay around *her*? "How long are you there for?"

"Six days. We leave on Wednesday."

We. Part of me hated how sure he was. And that was only a few days away. Most of me found it sexy. He was so confident and in control all the time. And apparently I was a sucker for an alpha male, if the growing moisture in my panties was any indication. "I don't know. Do you really think it's a good idea for us to be around each other?"

"You're mine and I want you with me. It's that simple."

My stomach tightened with a flicker of desire. I wanted to be with him, too. Wherever he was.

He reached across the table and took my hand. "I'm not tiptoeing around Fiona. She'll have to get used to us together, and I don't want to be without you, so I'm hoping for my sake that you'll come."

I nodded. "I'll think about it." I should probably stay in New York to be available for job interviews but I found myself giddy at the thought of escaping the dreary, cold weather in favor of a warm and tropical climate with him.

We didn't say anything for a long moment, just continued smiling at each other like two love-sick idiots. Ben broke the spell by chuckling and shaking his head.

"If I had known I'd be in a bikini in four days, I probably would have chosen a less fattening date for us tonight."

"Nonsense. Your body's perfect, baby. Eat up."

I loved how Ben appreciated my curves. Not that I needed his permission to enjoy this dessert. No way any of this was going to waste. "Chocolate's an aphrodisiac, you know?" I licked the droplet of warm, melted chocolate from my bottom lip then let my teeth graze the flesh there.

He watched me with a heated stare yet he remained poised and seemingly unaffected.

I upped the ante, slipping my shoe off under the table and bringing my foot to his lap.

His eyes were locked on my mouth and his Adam's apple bobbed as he swallowed. "Be careful, Emmy. I'll take you in the back and fuck you in the bathroom if you can't behave."

My heart thumped erratically in my chest and my body instinctively responded to the dark tone of his voice. It had been my idea to wait and now he was using it against me.

"You said you wanted to wait. Did you change your mind?"

I met his stare, my breathing suddenly hitching in my throat. "I-I'm not sure," I murmured.

"I know what you're trying to do," he said, his voice low and seductive.

"What's that?"

"The chocolate, the wine, the romance. You want me. It's okay, I understand." He treated me to one of his panty-melting smiles and I giggled nervously. "If you want me to fuck you, all you have to do is beg me."

Holy mother. I pressed my thighs together. I wouldn't beg him. Would I? But I pretty much broke every rule when it came to him. I'd jumped into bed and into this tumultuous relationship with him. I'd had a threesome with him and his friend simply because I couldn't stand the idea that Fiona had something I hadn't. My brain didn't work so well when I was near him. Logical thought went out the window, and instead I followed my body's instincts. Still, I couldn't believe how much he could turn me on with a heated stare and a bit of dirty talk. It really wasn't fair.

"Ben . . . that word . . ."

"Fuck?"

"Yeah. It's just so . . ."

"So, what?"

"Vulgar. Crass."

"If you want to be fucked raw, or make love, I'm happy to oblige whatever you want." He leaned closer, his intense, hazel gaze locked on mine. "But I seem to remember you liked it hard. I'm just trying to be helpful."

Blood rushed into my cheeks as my face heated. More like he was trying to kill me. I clamped my thighs together and straightened my spine, refocusing on the uneaten food on my plate.

Ben chuckled under his breath.

Soon after he paid the check and led me outside to where Henry was parked and waiting for us. Ben opened the passenger door and I slipped inside. I knew without asking that we'd be going to his place to spend the night. And I had no plans to argue with him over that.

Henry zipped away from the curb and Ben laced his fingers in mine.

7

Ben

When we reached my apartment I led Emmy inside, my hand resting against the small of her back. I flicked on the lights, giving my apartment a warm glow. Emmy settled on the couch while I gathered a bottle of red wine, a wine opener, and glasses from the kitchen. When I joined her on the couch I handed her a glass of the wine. I read the hesitation in her eyes that said she probably shouldn't have another, yet she took it. She hadn't directly answered me about Fiji but the interest in her eyes when I'd mentioned it was unmistakable. Though I'd hated how her first question had been about Fiona. I wanted to earn back her trust, but that single statement told me I hadn't.

"Cheers." I clinked my glass with hers. "To Fiji." I grinned crookedly, hoping she'd give me an answer this time.

Her mouth pursed down. "Ben."

"Yes, dear?" I smiled, innocently.

Emmy's mouth curved up like she couldn't help but smile at my expression.

"Will you come?"

Her eyes widened. "I said I'm thinking it over. Just give me some time." Her tone was low, serious. "I don't want to rush everything with us again."

I fisted my hands at my sides and released a slow exhale. Emmy, refusing to meet my eyes, set her untouched wineglass on the coffee table. Inside the restaurant she seemed open to the idea of joining me. Now it seemed, with a little more time to think it over, she was questioning things again. I didn't like the furrowed line in her forehead or the way her eyes drifted from mine. "Emmy, talk to me. Please." I smoothed my thumb across the crease in her brow.

She released a heavy sigh and met my eyes. "Time, Ben. That's all. It's going to take time." She rose to her feet. "And right now I need to go. I need to look for jobs."

What the hell?

"Now? It's . . ." I looked at my watch. "Ten thirty."

"Yes. Now." She grabbed her purse from beside the table and dashed to the door.

I caught her in the hall, lightly gripping her upper arms and turning her to face me. "Wait. If you need to go, at least let me call Henry."

She glanced at the floor between us. "No, it's fine. I'd prefer to take the train. It'll give me time to think."

She was out of my grasp and heading to the elevator before I had time to react. My legs jumped into action and

I pinned her against the wall where she stood. "Stop. Don't run from me, dammit. Tell me what's going on." Her refusal to meet my eyes, her sudden need to get away, both had my heart hammering in my chest. "What's this about? Why are you really leaving?"

"I'm going to the library in the morning. They're holding a career resources seminar that I want to attend at ten. I want to be in my own apartment to get ready in the morning. I already mapped out the train route to get me there."

"I'll have Henry take you to the library in the morning."

"I don't have clothes here."

"I have staff working for me, baby. I'll send them out to pick up whatever you need." As if I would have her go without.

She shook her head. "Ben, not everything revolves around you."

Until I felt like she was really back with me, I wouldn't let this go. I didn't like her keeping me at a distance. We were in this together. She needed to see that.

"I just don't want to do anything I might regret in the morning . . . and you tempt me," she admitted, her voice just a whisper.

She thought I wanted to take her to bed. She was right, but I wasn't about to force her. "When I fuck you again, I told you . . . it'll be because you're begging for it."

She whimpered and drew a shuddering breath.

Gliding my index and middle fingers into her mouth, Emmy sucked at them greedily, making my dick rise. Her eyes stayed on mine while her tongue drew circles around my digits. The gesture itself was innocent but we both knew what I wanted—to slide these fingers inside her hot, tight little opening.

I pulled my hand away and captured her mouth in a kiss. And not just any kiss. A tongue-probing-lip-crushing-I-want-to-fuck-you kiss. If she was going to turn me down, I would at least leave her with something to think about later. And her tingling lips and wet panties would ensure she'd be remembering me. Working my hand into the front of her pants, I pushed my fingers into her panties. Warm, soft, and wet. My dick lengthened and pushed against my zipper. "You say you don't want to fuck, but this pussy's nice and wet for me, baby."

Emmy groaned and buried her hands in my hair, pulling me back to her mouth. "No sex, Ben. Not yet."

I wondered if she was waiting to hear the results of my STD test, which had come back negative, or if she was just . . . waiting for some unknown point in the future. I saw no point in waiting. I knew I loved her, knew I wanted to be with her, but if it was what she wanted, I would respect it. Even if I did tease her a little.

I circled her clit, eliciting a tiny whimper from her, but she didn't stop me. I wondered if she'd use me for her orgasm and then leave. If that was the case, I had no problem with stroking my own dick until I came. I just wanted to touch her. To watch her get off.

Her hips pushed toward mine and when she felt my erection brush against her belly, a low moan tumbled from her parted lips. My fingers continued massaging her. Her pink cheeks and stuttering breaths told me she was close.

Suddenly aware that we were still in the hallway, I ripped my hand free from her pants and hauled her inside my apartment. I would make damn sure no one got to hear Emmy when she came. Her moaning out my name was the best sound in the world. And only I was entitled to hear it.

Once we were back inside I didn't allow Emmy the chance to change her mind. I needed to touch her like I needed my next breath. It had been too long. I'd prefer to watch her strip off her clothes piece by piece and let me kiss and taste her skin, but I'd settle for a quick orgasm if that was all I'd get from her tonight.

Unbuttoning her pants and pulling them down to her knees, I ripped the panties from her body, discarding the scrap of lace beside us on the floor. "Sorry. I hope those weren't your favorite pair."

She raised an eyebrow. She knew I wasn't sorry. Not a bit.

I could smell the scent of her arousal, and my mouth watered to taste her. I pressed one hand flat against the wall next to her head and leaned closer to kiss her pretty mouth. Emmy returned my kiss; her warm tongue probing my mouth was the only encouragement I needed. I brought my free hand between us and found her silken folds. She was shaved bare. Just the way I liked it so that all her hot flesh was exposed to my touch.

With each sweep of my fingers over her clit Emmy groaned. Her breathing grew shaky and I knew she was close.

I slid one finger inside her, pushing it in and dragging it out slowly.

"Bennn . . ."

My cock responded to her husky voice, a warm droplet of fluid leaking from the tip.

When I felt her clench around my finger and begin to tremble I removed my hand and pressed both against the wall behind her, caging her in.

"Ben?" She was breathless. "I was about to . . ."

"I know."

Her brows drew together. "Why'd you stop?"

It was a manipulative-asshole move but I needed her to understand our relationship was deeper than a quick romp against the wall in my entryway. Emmy needed to see that. And if she didn't, I would show her. "Stay the night with me. I'll happily finish this in my bed with you undressed beneath me."

Her expression changed from one of passionate desire to confusion in a heartbeat's time. "You're denying my orgasm to con me into staying with you?"

"No, baby. Of course not." My voice turned sweet, soft, and I stroked her cheek with my knuckle. "I want to give you everything and more. You just have to let me."

She blinked up at me, thinking it over. Determination blazed in her eyes and her teeth sunk into her bottom lip. Emmy gripped my right wrist and brought my fingers into the warm cavern of her mouth, surprising me. She swirled her tongue and sucked at them in a way that had all my attention.

Then she slid my fingers from her mouth and lowered my hand to her still-damp sex. Her little nub was swollen and distended and I knew she needed release, but I wouldn't have imagined she'd demand it this way—to use my own fingers against me. But that was exactly what she was doing. I let my hand go limp, allowing her to move it as she wished. She pressed my fingers against her clit, rubbing the pads of my fingers in slow circles that quickly increased in pace as her body responded.

Tiny whimpers fell from her lips and her pelvis rocked forward in time with my hand's movement.

As much as I'd wanted to prove a point between us tonight, I was powerless to remove my hand from her grip. Watching Emmy get herself off was insanely fucking hot. Her chest rose and fell with her quick inhalations until suddenly she sucked in a breath and held it, coming on my hand. I pushed two fingers inside her clenching sex muscles. She released a low moan, her body going limp as her orgasm subsided. I had never wanted to fuck her more, seeing this version of Emmy—confident, in control, and so sexual. It was maddening. I held her in place while little tremors pulsed through her limp body.

Once the aftershocks subsided she released a contented sigh and pulled her pants back into place and fastened them. "Don't play games with me or try to deny me." Her voice was surprisingly composed. She pressed a chaste kiss to my lips.

I stood there dumbfounded, wondering what this sexual

creature had done with my sweet, eager-to-please southern belle.

She reached out and gave my erection a gentle squeeze. "Good night."

I watched her walk out the door, the sway in her hips confident, almost cocky.

I dropped my head, rubbing a hand over the back of my neck. Her torn panties lay on the floor at my feet. Like Cinderella leaving a slipper behind, the scrap of lace was my only evidence she'd been here at all.

Unable to process what had just happened between us, I retreated to my room, falling back heavily onto the bed. I was still rock-hard and turned on, and I knew I wouldn't be able to think clearly until that was attended to.

Freeing myself from the confines of my pants, I stroked my dick in fast, uneven strokes until I came. Milky white fluid spilled onto my clenched abdominals in a matter of minutes.

The score was Emmy one, Ben zero. I needed to change that. Laying there breathless and confused, an idea struck me. A solution to all this. It looked like I'd be paying a visit to her roommate Ellie tomorrow to settle a few things.

8

Ben

When I arrived in Queens that morning a quick check of the clock told me that Emmy should be at the library for her seminar. I pressed the button for their intercom, hoping her roommate was home.

"Yeah?" Ellie said a moment later.

"Hey, it's Ben. Can I come up for a minute?"

"Um, Emmy's not home."

"I know. I wanted to talk to you alone, actually."

"Oh." Her confusion was evident in her tone, even through the scratchy intercom speaker. "Okay. Come on up. I'll buzz you in."

I took the stairs to apartment 4B. The aroma of various international cuisines hit my nostrils inside the building, along with the smell of damp, sour laundry from the first-floor laundry room.

When I reached their unit Ellie was standing in the doorway waiting for me. "Well, look who it is . . . the man, the legend, Mr. Ben Shaw." She smiled sarcastically. "What brings you by?"

"I was hoping we could talk about a few things concerning Emmy."

"Sure." She waved me inside after her and closed the door. "You want anything to drink?"

"I'm fine, thank you." We headed toward the one small sofa dominating their living room and sat down.

"So . . ." Ellie cocked her head, waiting for me to explain my presence here.

"I'd like Emmy to move in with me. I know she's worried about finding a job and paying rent here. She could work for me and live with me to take care of both problems."

"That's a bit sudden, don't you think?"

I shrugged. "Not when I know we belong together. I don't take this lightly. I've never lived with a woman; I've never even considered it. Emmy has challenged everything I thought I knew about relationships. I want this. And it has nothing to do with her being late on her rent, either."

Ellie's expression softened. "Why are you telling this to me and not her?"

"Because I know her and how determined she is to make her own way. She might require some convincing, a gentle nudge in the right direction."

"You want me to help you convince Emmy to move in with you and what, be your personal sex slave?" She raised her brows, taunting me. "Sounds like a demanding position."

"No. I'd like her to be my assistant. And yes, when I talk to her about all this I assume she'll ask your opinion. I was hoping you'd see things my way."

Ellie looked skeptical.

"I've also taken the liberty of hiring a roommate-finding service for you. They advertise the room opening, interview applicants for you, and complete background checks on potential tenants. You would have your rent covered here."

Her eyes lit up and locked on mine. I could tell I'd just hit on a key point. I'd known that Ellie was working overtime to cover both shares of their rent. And now that I was paying attention, I noticed her skin was pale and dark circles underscored her eyes. She looked worn out.

"If she brings it up to me, I'll talk to her. But I'm not going to convince her to do something she doesn't want to do."

I nodded. "Okay. I understand." I wasn't going to force Emmy into this arrangement, either. But if she worked for me, she'd be free to join me in Fiji and any other place I was working. I needed her with me. Plain and simple. And Emmy had immensely enjoyed her travels in Paris and Milan. This would be a chance for her to see the world.

I rose to leave, wanting to be gone by the time Emmy arrived home. "Thanks, Ells."

"Ells. I like that." She patted the top of my head like a dog. "Maybe you're not such a bad guy after all."

I chuckled as I exited the apartment. Maybe one day I'd win her over.

Emmy

I was exhausted when I arrived home. I wanted out of the dress clothes and to slip into a warm bath. I'd fought the cold winter air blasting through New York and the subway system all for nothing. The seminar I'd attended was a complete waste of time. More than fifty of us sat in the audience, eager for practical advice and actual job leads while an ancient librarian talked about proper formatting of a résumé and how to use computers to apply for jobs online. I was a little more advanced than step-by-step instructions for attaching my résumé to an email.

Ellie was all smiles when I found her in the living room. "How'd it go?"

"Exhausting. I'm going to take a bath."

"Did you hear from Ben today?"

"No. Why?"

She shook her head. "No reason."

That was strange. I shrugged it off and headed into the bathroom to fill the tub. I considered pouring myself a glass of wine and bringing it into the bath with me, but seeing that it was only two in the afternoon I decided against it. It wasn't a habit I wanted to start.

After my bath I lounged on my bed with my laptop and was surprised to see an email from Ben pop into my inbox.

From: Ben Shaw

To: Emerson Clarke

Subject: Hot Assistant

To Whom it May Concern:

I am hoping that you can point me in the right direction. You see, I'm in desperate need of a hot and sexy assistant. The girl I'm looking for is about five feet three inches tall, has long brown hair, pretty gray eyes, a sassy mouth, and the most adorable southern accent. She's also a food pusher. Know of anyone that fits this description? I'm willing to pay handsomely to have her at my service.

Yours,

Bennn . . .

I read the email twice wondering if it was some kind of joke. I picked up my phone and called him.

"Hi, baby." The deep tone of his sexy voice still affected me. My heart kicked up a notch at the way the nickname rolled off his tongue.

"Hi. I was just reading your email."

"Oh yeah?"

"Yesss . . ." I drew out the word, suddenly feeling unsure.

He chuckled to himself, the rich sound reverberating through the phone, sending a shiver down my spine. "And?"

I sat up straighter in bed, removing the computer from my lap. "Were you being serious?"

"Of course."

"I can't take your money, Ben. I'd help you with anything you needed me to."

"Nonsense. What was Fiona paying you?"

I reluctantly told him.

"I'll double that."

"No way. That's way too much." I'd been paid decently by Status Model Management, and though living in New York was expensive, I'd never in my life expected to make as much money as he was offering me. He was insane.

"Emmy, don't argue with me."

I snapped my mouth shut even though he couldn't see me. He was so dominating, so in control. I felt powerless to disobey.

"Just listen for a moment," he continued.

I bit my cheek, waiting for him to continue.

"I want whatever this is between us. I want a real relationship with you. My job takes me all over the world. This won't work if we're separated for weeks on end. You know that."

I wondered if he doubted himself, or us, or if he knew he'd be tempted to stray if we were apart. My stomach cramped at the thought. "If I worked for you, what would I even do for you?"

"Manage my social media presence online, answer emails,

coordinate my bookings, arrange travel for us. Travel the world with me and have hot, sweaty sex on as many continents as we could check off the list."

"Ben."

"Yeah, baby?"

"Be serious."

"I am serious. I want you. I want you with me always. You need a job. I need an assistant. Why the fuck would I keep paying Gunnar and have his ass travel with me when I'd just be sitting there alone in a hotel, missing you? Think about it, Emmy."

I was quiet for a moment while I thought it over. His idea actually did make sense. We could be together. Really together. "What about Fiona? Would I have to deal with her if I worked for you?"

He released a heavy sigh. "Unfortunately I don't see a way around that one. But I can talk with her directly if you prefer not to."

I didn't know which was worse, having to deal directly with Fiona or the idea of Ben talking to her alone. I'd have to suck it up and deal with it. The idea of paying my half of the rent again was appealing. "I have to think about it."

He was silent for a moment. "There's something else, too."

"Oh?"

"I'd like you to move in with me. We'd be together most of the time anyway while traveling, during which Ellie would be practically living alone. She could get another roommate who's actually around. Safety in numbers and all that. And it'd put you right here with me, which is exactly what I want."

He'd made a solid argument, though moving in together was moving way too fast for my taste. "I'll think about it." I chewed on my thumbnail.

"Can I come pick you up? I could feed you dinner tonight and we could hang out."

"I was planning on staying in tonight. I haven't spent much time with Ellie." Everything around me was moving so fast, I didn't want to leave the solitude of my room, let alone the country.

"Fine. But promise me you'll think about everything and call me before you go to bed. I need to hear your voice."

A pang of guilt pressed down on me. I knew he didn't sleep well without me. But Ben had the ability to completely possess me, and that scared me. If I turned myself over to him too completely, jumped in all at once, I worried about what would happen when he was done with me. I already loved him with every fiber of my being, but if I also worked for him and lived with him . . . I needed to make sure I was still me. I couldn't allow myself to become crushed again or sink into a depression like I had when I had found out about him and Fiona's secret past and her pregnancy.

"I'll call you before bed," I confirmed.

"I love you, Emmy. You know that, right?" he said, his voice suddenly serious.

"I love you, too."

9

Emmy

Ben's offer weighed on my mind in the days that followed. I honestly wasn't sure what to do. He was leaving for Fiji tomorrow and I still hadn't answered him. I wanted to go with him more than anything. I was even warming to the idea of being his assistant. But as far as moving in with him, I wasn't so sure that was smart so early in our relationship.

He'd texted me this morning and asked if I would come over today, and when I said sure, he'd informed me that Henry was on his way. I didn't know if I'd ever get used to his lifestyle.

I pulled on my winter coat and I trudged through the snow to the waiting black sedan. Henry hopped out and opened the back door for me. "Don't you have any luggage?" His quizzical look roamed my empty hands. "For your trip to Fiji?"

"I haven't agreed to go yet." Geez. Did Ben even listen to anything I said? Apparently not if he'd already told his driver I was going.

"Oh, I'm sorry, Miss."

"It's okay, Henry. Shall we go?" It was freezing out.

"Of course." He helped me into the warm car and we rode in awkward silence to Ben's.

Arriving in Gramercy Park, I was once again struck by the quaint feel and beauty of this part of the city. Little lampposts and wrought iron fences, redbrick apartment buildings, and a fluffy white coating of snow made it feel like something out of a Norman Rockwell painting.

When I saw Ben, the anger I felt about being conned into this trip instantly faded.

He was bare chested, dressed in only a pair of loose athletic shorts that accentuated the deep V-cut of his obliques and his stunning six-pack abs. I wanted to lick those babies.

"Hey, sorry I'm all sweaty. I just got done working out." He pulled me close for a quick kiss on the lips before releasing me. Not fast enough, though, because I was still hit with the masculine scent of his musky, sweat-dampened skin. That smell reminded me of our last few weeks together in Paris. We'd spent every waking moment we could in bed, exploring each other's bodies. Memories of Ben's hot, large body draped over mine flooded my senses, and my sex muscles clenched automatically.

"Hi," I squeaked out.

His eyes traveled down his own naked chest and abs and

he chuckled under his breath, seeming to understand that just the sight of his perfect physique had me breaking out in chill bumps and flushing pink.

"Henry got you here faster than I expected. I just need to jump in the shower. Make yourself at home."

Home.

I nodded then watched him walk away, appreciating the powerful muscles in his back, and wondered if this could really be my home. I looked around at his beautiful apartment. It certainly felt comfortable and inviting, from the leather armchairs flanking the gas fireplace to the soft, upholstered sofa and thick rugs scattered across the wood floors. Not to mention the luxurious chef's kitchen that was a far cry from the tiny kitchen I'd grown up cooking in and the decadent bathroom outfitted in white marble with a steam shower and deep, sunken tub. Part of me wanted to say yes, to be daring and romantic and spontaneous. But in that moment, standing alone in the quiet solitude of his apartment, I realized I needed to have a safety net. I needed to have a place of my own to return to just in case things went south between us. Not that I expected them to, but even if I could see myself living here someday, I wasn't the type to rely solely on a man.

The sound of water from the bathroom caught my attention and I considered, for the briefest of moments, joining him in the shower. But seconds later the bathroom door opened and a haze of steam escaped. Ben stepped out wearing just a towel riding low on his hips.

"You okay, babe?" He stopped in his tracks, raising an eyebrow at me.

I realized I was still standing in the same spot he'd left me. I hadn't even sat down, let alone moved from the foyer.

I briefly wondered if I should feel embarrassed for my behavior the last time I was here, standing in this same entryway. I'd wantonly used Ben's hand against myself until I came. My body folding in on itself and my womb contracting around his fingers. But he didn't mention it, so neither did I.

"I'm fine," I murmured. "I've decided about a few of the things we, um, talked about." I didn't know why I felt like we were negotiating a business arrangement. I guess we were, with my impending employment.

"Good. Come in my room while I dress."

I followed him into the cozy room and sat on the end of his bed while Ben removed a stack of clothes from his bureau. He dropped the towel and my breathing hitched in my chest. My audible gasp in the silent room made Ben smile. God, his body was magnificent. A work of art. I'd never seen him not erect, but even in its relaxed state his length hung heavily between his legs. He stepped into black boxers, quickly concealing my view of the goods. My eyes snapped up to his and I smiled sheepishly.

He crossed the room and stood in front of me with dewy skin, looking hotter than hell. "See something you like?" He leaned down over me, planting his hands on either side of the bed near my thighs.

I sucked in a breath and held it. He smelled clean, like soap and aftershave. I nodded slowly, not letting my eyes wander from his. If I looked down at his beautifully tempting body, I might do something I hadn't bargained for, like grab ahold of him and not let go.

"Tell me what you've decided, beautiful." He reached toward me and stroked my cheek, his long finger lingering near my mouth.

"Henry expected me to have luggage packed for Fiji." I frowned.

"Will you come with me?"

"I was considering it but I don't like that you just assumed I'd go and told your driver that I was."

His hand dropped to mine and he laced our fingers together. "I gave Henry my updated schedule to let him know I wouldn't need his services while I was away. I mentioned I'd be in Fiji and that I'd invited you to join me. He must have assumed that you'd said yes."

"Oh." His explanation did make sense.

"*Oh.*" He gave my hand a gentle squeeze and a smile twitched on his lips. Dropping my hand to rest in my lap, he continued getting dressed, slipping into dark jeans and a long-sleeved gray T-shirt.

"Can I get you a glass of wine and you can tell me the rest of what's on your mind?"

"Sure." I let him guide me into the kitchen, his fingertips pressing lightly into my lower back. I lingered by the kitchen island while Ben opened a bottle of white wine. "Chateau Ste. Michelle Riesling." He held up the green bottle for me to see. "It's sweet, just like you."

I accepted the glass he offered, little dots of condensation already forming on the goblet.

"Are you ready to tell me what's on your mind? I think you've left me in the dark about your feelings long enough."

I nodded. He led the way to the living room. "I don't like feeling pressured into making a decision," I said once we were seated together on the sofa.

His eyes lifted to mine. "I never meant to pressure you, but before you answer, there's something I need to say." He hesitated a moment, peering down into his wineglass. "You know my background. It's not something I talk about with very many people. I never knew my dad, I was raised by a single mom who took off for months at a time when it suited her, so I'm sorry to put added pressure on you, but I need you to understand I don't handle rejection well."

His raw honesty surprised me. It wasn't what I expected him to say. I remained silent for several moments, taking in what he'd just told me. He'd be hurt if I refused his offer. The last thing I wanted to do was reject him. From the beginning I'd wanted to care for him, soothe him, and I understood now that he was putting himself out on the line—not only by inviting me on his next assignment but by offering me a job and his home as well. This was a big step for him.

"Ben, I will happily work for you. But the pay you proposed is too much."

He watched me intently, waiting for me to continue.

"And as your assistant and your girlfriend," I smiled at the word, "of course I'll go to Fiji."

"But you won't move in?" he asked, his eyes reading the indecision in mine.

"No." I swallowed. "Not yet, anyway. I like having my own space. I came to New York intent on paving my own way, and I met Ellie and we really clicked. I'm not ready to give all that up just yet. I hope you understand. It has nothing to do with you."

He nodded. "Okay. It's something to build up to." He leaned in close and pressed a sweet kiss to my lips.

"We leave tomorrow, right? I should probably go home and pack."

He shook his head, kissing me again. "Not necessary," he mumbled against my lips. "I already packed a bag for you."

I laughed. "Really? It's probably nothing but frilly panties and maybe a sex toy, knowing you."

"I guess you'll have to wait and see." He kissed down my throat, roaming over to the side of my neck to nibble at the skin below my ear, and I shuddered involuntarily, forgetting all about packing.

10

Emmy

After a six-hour flight to Los Angeles we boarded a twelve-hour flight to Fiji. Luckily I slept most of the way with my head resting on Ben's shoulder. My neck was stiff and sore when I finally awoke. Sparkling turquoise water as far as the eye could see greeted me out the window. Ben leaned over to look with me. "Wow. It's so pretty." He kissed my temple. "I haven't received my schedule for the shoots yet but hopefully we have time to play."

I turned to face him. "As your assistant should I be emailing someone to find out your schedule?"

He shrugged. "Sure. If you'd like."

"Ben," I scolded. "I'm not okay with being your assistant in title only. I will work hard for you. We should actually discuss all this—your expectations, needs, what my role will be."

"Baby, I'm not worried about it. Just having you with me helps me."

I clamped my mouth closed. I could see that it would be up to me to determine my role as an assistant. He wasn't going to boss me around or give me any direction. I pulled out my cell phone and powered it on while the plane taxied to the gate.

"What are you doing?" Ben asked.

"Checking if I can get a Wi-Fi connection here."

"You should near the airport, in the populated areas, and at our hotel, but I'm not sure about the rest of the island. Why?"

"Does Fiona know I'm your assistant?"

"Not yet."

Oh boy. "She's about to."

Ben smiled at my confidence.

Seeing that I had cell phone service, I quickly typed out my message.

To: Fiona Stone
From: Emmy Clarke
Subject: Fiji Shoots

Fiona,

Can you please send me Ben's schedule of all bookings while we are here in Fiji? We'd like to know what is planned for the duration of the trip.

Thank you,

Emmy Clarke

Assistant to Ben Shaw

Ha! That ought to give her something to think about.

"If you'd like me to manage your social media presence, like Gunnar used to, I'll just need your passwords for the sites you'd like me to help with."

"Sure. That'd be great."

I could post behind-the-scenes pictures of his shoots. His fans would appreciate seeing snippets of those.

"Excellent." I felt more in control and confident about my role already.

Stepping off the plane, I realized I was in desperate need of a shower. I wanted to wash my face and my limp, greasy hair and change out of the rumpled jeans and T-shirt I'd been wearing for a solid eighteen hours. After collecting our luggage Ben and I moved toward the airport exit where I spotted a uniformed driver holding a sign that read *Ben Shaw*. I poked him in the side with my elbow and pointed.

"Fiona must have arranged a pickup. I was planning to grab a cab."

Oh, Fiona. How lovely. God, I was really going to have to keep my temper in check. I was here in my own right this time, and she couldn't just send me packing. I straightened my shoulders and followed the driver and Ben.

Once outside the humidity smacked me in the face. My hair instantly increased in volume. I blinked against the sunlight and took in our surroundings—a tiny little airport surrounded by massive palm trees.

I slid into the white limousine, which was really quite ridiculous for two people, while Ben assisted the driver with placing our bags inside the trunk.

This was my first visit to the South Pacific and I was in awe of the idyllic setting, crystal-blue waters, brilliant blue and cloudless sky, tropical flowers and plants, and rolling hills in the distance. Everything was lush and green. Vibrant, and so pretty.

The driver stopped in front of a pink-and-white stucco hotel. It was charming, but somewhat understated, letting the natural beauty of the island stand out.

We headed inside and I felt out of place in my jeans and T-shirt, which would've been fine back home. Here I felt homely and anything but sophisticated. The lobby was little more than a large, thatched roof pitched over marble floors. It was open on all sides, allowing the ocean breeze to lift strands of hair from my neck and providing a breathtaking view of the beach beyond.

We were handed cocktails poured into real coconuts while we checked in. I sipped the icy, sweet concoction, letting the flavors of spiced rum and creamy coconut milk dance on my tongue while Ben handed over his credit card. I could get used to this life.

The approach of clicking heels across the marble floor caught my attention and I turned.

Fiona was here.

She was island perfection in a colorful pastel sundress and gold sandals. Her dress was loose fitting but her belly had grown since I'd seen her last. Her skin was lightly tanned and she was glowing.

Fuck me.

I wished I could stop comparing myself to this woman but knowing she'd had a five-year affair with my boyfriend made that a teensy bit hard to do.

"Love! You made it!" She had eyes only for Ben and threw herself into his arms.

"Fiona." Ben greeted her coolly and removed her claws from around his waist.

Her eyes landed on mine. "Oh. Emerson. I didn't expect to see you."

Ben's arm came around my waist, drawing me closer. "Emmy's staying with me, and I'd appreciate it if you'd cooperate with her."

Fiona's answering smile was as fake as they came, her lips curving up to reveal too-white teeth. "Of course, my love. I'll play nice." One hand moved to rest against her belly.

"Hi, Fiona." I found my voice, however soft and shaky. "I emailed you about obtaining Ben's schedule while we're here."

"I'll send it to him tonight."

"Send it to Emmy," Ben interrupted.

"Of course," she said, looking slightly wounded. "We have a pre-production dinner tonight with the photographer," she added.

"Emmy's working for me now so it'll be good for her to hear whatever's discussed tonight."

"She's working *for* you?" Fiona's brow crinkled, the frown lines around her mouth puckering like she'd tasted something sour.

"Yes. She's my assistant." Ben's fingers dug into my hip as his grasp on me tightened.

"How . . . *cute*." The word "cute" dripped with sarcasm. *Bitch.*

"We're just getting checked in, if you'll excuse us," Ben said.

"I booked your room next to mine, like we usually do. I'll see you soon," Fiona said before sauntering away.

Ben and I were both silent as a bellhop led us to our room. I hoped it wouldn't continue to feel this tense the entire time we were here. And if there was an adjoining door to Fiona's room, I was going to lose it.

The hotel was quite elegant, so there were no adjoining doors. I quickly became distracted by and fascinated with our room, which was actually a large suite. I spent a solid twenty minutes exploring while sipping my yummy coconut and rum drink. A plush living room decorated in island furniture led to the master bedroom with a king-sized bed draped in a white, gauzy canopy and French doors that gave way to a private terrace and view of the ocean.

"Is everything to your liking, Miss Clarke?" Ben's deep voice rushed over my skin, making me tingle from head to toe.

I spun to face him, abandoning my inspection of the vase of exotic flowers placed artfully on the dresser. "It's lovely."

He took the empty coconut from my hands, set it on the nearby dresser, and pulled me into his arms. "Thank you for being here."

"Thank you for inviting me," I murmured, getting lost in the intensity of his hazel gaze.

"Just think, six days here together. . . ."

"I've got quite a demanding boss to keep happy."

"It's the other way around, babe. I'll gladly do anything and everything to make you happy."

"Well, thank you for sticking up for me with Fiona and telling her I work for you."

"Hmm . . . I think being the boss should entitle me to some perks." He slid one finger under the hem of my T-shirt and traced a tiny circle against my hip bone.

I barely resisted the urge to squirm under his soft, languid touch that promised so much more. "Such as?"

"I get to tell you what to do. All of my desires, all my requests, will be in your hands to fulfill." The dark, predatory look in his eyes made my breath catch in my throat.

"And what do you want?"

His hand slid lower and caressed my bottom as he drew me closer. Leaning in, his mouth brushed against my earlobe and his warm breath sent my pulse racing. "I want to strip you naked, lay you on the bed, spread you open, and taste you until you come," he whispered against my skin.

Okay, clearly we were going to have to talk about the proper etiquette of being my employer. He was a walking, talking human resources nightmare. Good thing I had no plans to turn him in for sexual harassment. I pulled back just a fraction. "What if I'm not so keen on fucking my boss?" I licked my lips and his gaze zeroed in on my mouth.

His thumb stroked my bottom lip. "Or I could order you to your knees and put this pretty mouth to use."

His large palm continued lightly rubbing my ass, and I swear just that simple touch and the burning desire I saw reflected in his eyes was making me wet. "I wanted to be gentle, make love to you properly, but you're making that impossible. The longer you make me wait, the harder I'm going to fuck you when you do finally give in."

"Ben . . . we have to get ready for your pre-production dinner. I need to shower, dry my hair. . . ."

"We'll discuss this later," he said, and gave my butt a playful swat.

I yelped at the unexpected contact and absently massaged the heated spot as I made my way to the bathroom for a shower.

After a long, hot shower, I wrapped myself in the downy hotel robe and padded into the bedroom in search of the suitcase Ben had packed for me.

I was surprised to find so many pretty and elegant things inside. A basic black string bikini, a pink-and-white polka-dotted bikini with a matching pale pink sarong, casual flip-flops, espadrille wedges, several sundresses—all designer brands and each in my size. There were shorts, skirts, and tank tops in every color. I selected a pretty royal blue strapless sundress and a pair of silver strappy sandals with little jewels at the ankles. There was even a little pewter-colored handbag that I could tuck a tube of lip gloss into at least. I laid out the dress and finished getting ready, blow-drying my hair and applying light makeup.

When I slipped on the dress I found it was a perfect fit. It hugged my every curve and landed just above my knees. I straightened the bodice that gently squeezed my breasts and inspected myself in the mirror one last time.

"You look beautiful, baby." Ben's hands slid across my hips and settled against my waist.

I loved getting dressed up for him. It had a way of making me feel pretty and put together. I knew it was foolish but just the fact that this beautiful man found me worthy of being on his arm made me feel confident. Stepping into the silver-jeweled sandals, I felt like Cinderella, and the glass slipper even fit.

Ben

Strolling into the restaurant with Emmy on my arm made me feel both comfortable and uneasy. Comfortable because she had a way about her that made me feel relaxed and calm. Uneasy because we were preparing to be around Fiona. Who could possibly be carrying my baby, and who was known to treat Emmy like shit. I was leading her into shark-infested waters. All my senses were up.

We were the first two to be seated at the table for four on the expansive terrace that overlooked the turquoise-blue water. I helped Emmy into her chair and couldn't help but notice she was fidgeting. Toying with the little strap on her purse and spinning the silver bracelet on her wrist.

"Hey, we've got this. I'll take care of you. Always. You trust me, right?"

Pretty gray eyes locked on mine and she gave me a careful nod.

The server appeared, a slight young girl who seemed captivated by me. Great. Just what I needed. I didn't want

Emmy feeling insecure. I reached across the table and took her hand. I cleared my throat and the waitress's gaze snapped up. "Something to drink?"

"Yes, just water for me please, but what beers do you have on tap?" I nodded to Emmy.

Emmy's lips curved in a smile as she listened to the choices, and then placed her order. I knew my girl.

Once the server was gone, Emmy shot me a curious glance. "Water because of your shoots coming up?"

I nodded. It actually wasn't, but letting her think so was easier. I wanted all my wits about me to deflect Fiona's cruelty from Emmy tonight. I didn't want alcohol slowing my reaction time or numbing me to the situation. This was essentially the first time they would be forced into each other's company, and frankly that scared the hell out of me. I would need to play interference. I wouldn't have Fiona belittling my girl.

The evening breeze picked up strands of Emmy's hair and lifted them from her neck. I watched her, mesmerized, until a wave of laughter with a British accent interrupted our silence. My stomach cramped. My new girlfriend and my ex-lover at the same table. *Fuck.*

Emmy

Fiona strolled onto the terrace in a flowing orange sundress on the arm of an older bald man, who I assumed was our company for the evening. She looked gorgeous, as always, and I hated her for it. While my hair was three times its normal volume and frizzed out of control from the humidity, hers was flat-iron sleek and smooth and hung in a glossy wave down her back. Her lips were painted in pink gloss, and were those false eyelashes? I resisted rolling my eyes and instead followed Ben's lead, standing to greet them both.

She kissed Ben on both cheeks and I clenched my fists so tightly my nails cut into my palms. Ouch. *Breathe, Emmy,* I reminded myself.

The bald man introduced himself as Gentry Smith. He was the photographer for the photo shoot.

Once we'd ordered drinks, Fiona stood from the table, one hand resting on her little swollen belly. "Will you excuse me a moment? I need to visit the loo. This baby makes me wee more." She chuckled.

Whore.

I had no patience for her or this pregnancy. If that made me a terrible person, so be it. I was trying my damnedest to be polite and well mannered around her. I couldn't also be expected to control my thoughts. And in my mind, I'd clawed her eyes out before the appetizer even arrived.

We dined on grilled swordfish, tiger prawns, and scallop mousse, which I didn't think I'd like until Ben urged me to try a bite from his fork. I found it surprisingly good. But my favorite dish of the night was the garlic and Parmesan risotto. It was creamy and salty and I ate every bite on my plate.

I did my best to ignore Fiona, which was relatively easy. I focused on the delicious food as Gentry talked endlessly about all the models he'd shot over the years. It was poor taste, really, to brag as much as he did, but none of us minded because I sensed that Ben and Fiona were just as glad for the distraction as I was. He only talked briefly of their photo shoot on the beach, and I'd asked a few basic questions about his start and end times, like any good assistant would, before the topic was changed to covering the rest of Gentry's impressive list of accomplishments.

For being pregnant, Fiona didn't seem to have much of an appetite. She merely pushed the food around her plate, playing with it more than eating. For dessert, though, she requested pink grapefruit salad, and though I'd wanted the cheesecake I kept my trap shut and nodded along, ordering the same.

Ben leaned toward me. "Are you sure that's all you want?"

"Yes, that's fine," I answered.

He frowned, the crease in between his brows deepening as he studied me. He knew me too well.

Ben's left hand remained on my knee throughout the meal, his thumb softly caressing my skin. A few times I caught Fiona's gaze slipping back and forth between me and Ben and I wondered if she was pondering what he saw in me. I couldn't say I really felt bad for her; it was more like a subtle awareness permeating the air, reminding us all that he'd picked me and not her.

His hand crept higher up my thigh, his fingertips pressing into my flesh. Lifting my chin to look into his eyes, I saw a man in need. His intense hazel gaze was locked on mine and a shiver zipped up my spine. I had no idea what he was trying to tell me. Only that he seemed to need something. I fought to quiet the anxieties plaguing my mind.

He'd completely tuned out Gentry's rambling. His gaze was glued to my thighs where the sundress had hitched up when I'd sat down, and his fingertips traced little circles along the tender skin. His eyes were dark and hungry, almost primal in his craving for me. I pushed my knees together, trying to stop the little darts of pleasure racing up from his touch and making my panties feel constrictive over my sensitized flesh.

He'd been so attentive, so loving that I was starting to feel guilty making him wait so long. We'd already been intimate, already breached that boundary—many, many times in fact. But now because of the whole Fiona pregnancy fiasco, I'd sworn off sex with him. It probably wasn't fair for him. Or for me. Maybe I would change that tonight.

After dinner Ben led me inside our darkened hotel room, pressing my back against the door and taking my face in his hands. I tried to decipher the meaning in his haunted gaze but suddenly his mouth was crashing against mine, his lips firm and demanding. I parted my lips and his warm tongue sought entrance, sucking at mine greedily. His mouth moved down my throat, licking and stroking the skin with his tongue. Pressing his hips to mine, I felt the evidence of his arousal and I brought my hands up to his chest, my nails lightly raking over his firm pecs and abs. Moving his mouth from my skin, Ben captured my wrists and pinned them above my head. "Don't touch me if you're not going to finish the job, sweetheart."

Holding my hands against the door, Ben pushed his erection into my belly and a raw whimper escaped my throat. His eyes were filled with desire, and when he pressed into me I felt the rigid lines of his body, smelled the crisp sent of his cologne, and heat pooled between my legs.

"Fuck," he cursed loudly, dropping my wrists and turning away from me. He stormed across the room, both hands raking through his hair, and slammed the bathroom door behind him.

Whoa.

What had I done to set him off tonight?

Crossing the room on shaky legs, I paused at the sofa to

remove my strappy sandals and then padded barefoot across the marble floor. I knocked tentatively at the bathroom door. "Ben?"

Silence.

"Is everything okay?" I asked.

"Just fucking dandy," he answered, his voice tight.

Sheesh. I didn't know what started his temper tantrum but I was near certain I hadn't done anything wrong. "Ben, please talk to me." I tried the door handle and found it unlocked. Pushing the door open slowly, I found him leaning over the sink, his hands gripping the marble countertop, his head dropped forward.

My stomach twisted nervously. My mind jumped to the worst-case scenario. . . . Was he racked with guilt over something else he needed to confess about him and Fiona? Heaven help me because I knew I couldn't take it. And I was eighteen hours from home.

I wanted to ease his anxieties, to tell him that whatever it was we'd get through it, but I couldn't form the words. Instead I waited, twisting the bracelet on my wrist. Finally he turned.

"I can't do this."

My stomach dropped. God, why had I thought it was a good idea to eat scallop mousse? It was threatening to make an appearance.

He stepped closer, towering over me in my bare feet. "I can't share this room with you, sleep in the same bed, and be expected not to touch you. I love you, Emmy. You're mine. All of you. Your heart, mind, and body. And I'm yours."

"W-what are you saying?" I stammered.

"I just can't take it anymore," he said, releasing a heavy sigh filled with pent-up frustration.

"You don't want me?" I asked.

He laughed. The bastard actually laughed, a rich throaty chuckle that tumbled from his perfect mouth. "I've had the biggest case of blue balls since we got back together. I'm about to make the fucking *Guinness Book of World Records*. I'll have to see a doctor to make sure this won't cause permanent damage in case you want kids someday."

My heart swelled. He'd never discussed wanting children, and I suddenly found his little tantrum incredibly cute.

His hand unconsciously went to the bulge in his pants and he winced as he adjusted himself.

My eyes followed his movement. *Oh*. Heavens, that thing took my breath away. Had he escaped to the bathroom to deal with that on his own? Was that what this was about?

Everything struck me at once. Ben wanted me. He loved me. He needed this—to be intimate with me, for me to accept him and all his baggage. And I was denying him.

Bringing my hand toward him, I lightly rubbed his manhood through the thin material of his dress pants. His eyes flicked to mine and a low growl rumbled through his chest.

"You need me to kiss it and make it better?" I whispered.

His breathing faltered in his chest. "Don't tease me, baby. I can't take it."

A slow smile curled on my mouth. I was ready. And not just because of his pouty tantrumlike behavior. Even at dinner I'd questioned myself, and now alone with him in this room it was obvious. I wanted him, too. All of him. He was right, he was mine and I was his. There was no sense in waiting any longer. I worked to free his belt, taking my time pulling it from the loops while my eyes danced on his.

"Baby, stop, stop." His hands held mine, preventing me from pulling down his zipper. "Not like this. Not because you feel pressured."

I shook my head. "That's not it."

He pushed a lock of stray hair from my face, cupping my cheek. "Seriously, I'll take a cold shower and sleep on the couch. I'm not letting you do something you don't want. You wanted to wait. And we will."

"I'm done waiting."

His Adam's apple bobbed as he swallowed. "What brought that on?" he asked.

"Because." I leaned forward and pressed a kiss to his mouth. "I'm a woman. And I'm emotional and sometimes unsure and I change my mind about things. A lot." I kissed him again, his bottom lip jutting out the tiniest bit in a pout. "And I've decided. I'm ready." *Kiss.* "For this. For you. Us." *Kiss.*

Still cupping my face in his big, warm palms, his thumb lightly stroked my cheek. "Are you sure about this? I told you I can't take it if you're just playing around."

"Don't pout," I scolded him, pulling my hands from his hold so I could free his button and tug down his zipper.

He dutifully dropped his hands to his sides. Good boy. He was going to cooperate. I understood my changing moods may be giving him whiplash, but I really was ready, despite his sudden hesitation. Tugging his pants and boxer briefs down over his hips, Ben's hands went to rest on the top of his head and he looked down at me in wonder, his lips parting slightly.

I dropped to my knees in the ultimate submissive gesture. Pulling the material the rest of the way down his thighs, his cock sprang free, leaping to greet me. I'd forgotten how big he was. My skin heated at the sight of him and my mouth watered to taste him, to please him. He was swollen and had a thick vein pulsing along his shaft. Wrapping my fist around his long, thick cock, Ben let out a strangled moan. Apparently he wasn't going to last long tonight. I'd kept him waiting too long. A few simple touches and he was nearly there.

Hands fisted and still resting on top of his head, he pushed his hips forward, invading my mouth deeply. I accommodated his length, sliding my mouth all the way down until my lips were around his base. His knees locked and his entire body clenched in response. I loved pleasing him like this. Even though I was the one on my knees, submitting to him, I felt sexy and powerful.

His hands moved to my jawline and he cupped my face as he pulled himself free. "You're going to make me come already."

I smiled up at him, my lips swollen and my knees protesting from the unforgiving marble floor. Ben lifted me up under my arms and didn't stop until he'd placed me on the countertop so that I was facing him. In this position we were nearly the same height, and he pressed his lips to mine. "I need to be inside you, baby. I need to fuck you."

Without waiting for my response, his hands pushed under my dress and tugged at the lace thong I was wearing. I felt it being dragged across my knees, while Ben kissed me deeply. His fingers parted me and he pressed one long digit inside. I broke from the kiss to let out a soft moan.

"Fuck. You're soaking wet, baby." He brought the finger to his mouth and sucked it greedily, tasting me, and I saw his cock twitch between us the second his mouth closed around his finger. He stroked himself a few times and stepped in between my thighs, spreading me open. Guiding himself to my opening, Ben pressed forward. His mouth crashed against mine in a hungry kiss.

As his length slid inside me exquisitely, slowly, his head dropped back and a low groan slipped from his mouth. The sound was raw with pleasure. It ignited all my senses and I clenched around him. Gripping my hips, Ben slammed into me faster, harder, until the sounds of wet flesh slapping together was amplified in the small room. He fucked me hard and without any mercy, my first orgasm crashing through me in a sudden rush of heat.

"Fuck . . . I forgot how good your pussy is. Fuck. *Fuckkk.*" Unexpectedly, he pulled out and stroked himself until he came all over my pink flesh with a groan and then pushed back inside of me. The juices he'd marked me with made him slide in and out so deeply it stole my breath.

"Ben." My hand flattened on his clenched abs. "That's really deep . . ."

He slowed his pace, dragging himself in and out of me slowly, and brought his lips to mine. "I want you to feel me deep inside you, baby. All of me."

He pushed all the way in until we were no longer two separate people but one being, sharing eye contact, moving together, breathing in the same air. The rush of sensations was almost too much. I sucked in a lungful of air and held it, releasing it slowly.

"Your pussy belongs to me."

I dropped my hand, no longer wanting him to hold back. I needed all of him. I loved the way he owned me so completely. Once I gave myself over to the sensations and let go of control, it felt amazing. He was stretching me, filling me completely, but I loved it. "Faster . . . babe . . . I'm almost there . . ." I arched my back, pushing my hips closer to his. My second release blossomed deep inside me. I clutched his shoulders and hung on tight as he pounded into me.

"You're mine," he breathed. "Just mine."

"Always" I whispered.

Ben lifted me from the countertop and I wrapped my legs around his waist. One arm gripped around my bottom and his other hand settled on the back of my neck, pressing my mouth to his. Without breaking our connection, he walked us over to the bed and laid me down gently, momentarily pulling free from my body while he arranged a pillow under my head. I whimpered at the loss of him. I'd already come twice, and him once, but the look in Ben's eyes told me we were far from done. The hungry, possessive look I saw reflected in his gaze heated my skin and made my pulse jump erratically.

He joined me on the bed, lying over the top of me to cage me in against the mattress. He cradled my face in his hands, lowering his mouth to mine and mumbling soothing words in between sweet kisses. "I'm sorry, baby. I meant to go slow. I wanted to take my time with you and make you feel good."

He was apologizing? I supposed the bathroom counter wasn't the most romantic place to have sex, but I wasn't complaining. Not at all. I felt his erection nudging against my belly and I squirmed underneath him, trying to angle us closer.

Ben brushed stray strands of hair from my forehead and planted a soft kiss there. "I need to make love to you," he whispered in his deep, sexy voice.

I merely nodded. I hadn't heard him use those words before. Usually his language was much cruder, favoring the F-word for our physical act. I'd always felt there was more between us, even from the very beginning when I knew I shouldn't fall for him. I had. Totally and completely, and despite all the things fighting against us, I wanted him. Needed him. This man had consumed me and there was no denying that fact. I climbed on top of him, wanting to show him we were really okay. His body joined mine and the slow, sweet way he made love to me filled my entire heart and soul with so much emotion, I had to hang on to his biceps tightly to keep from combusting in happiness.

I rhythmically rode him, lifting up and gliding down so

slowly I could feel each inch of him invade me. Sensations blossomed deep inside me each time he was fully seated. The pace was agonizingly slow, but he let me maintain it. His hands moved to my hips, lifting and lowering me against him, and I loved the feel of his strength, commanding my body to do as he pleased. And he knew exactly what he was doing.

Ben

The sound of someone knocking on the door woke me from a deep slumber. Lifting Emmy from the spot she'd claimed on my chest, I gently placed her beside me and pulled off the blankets and rose to my feet.

Emmy rolled into the spot I'd vacated and pulled my pillow into her arms. She curled her legs up until she was hugging the pillow in a full-body embrace. Damn, that was one lucky pillow. She let out a sleepy little murmur. Just as I considered crawling back into bed, the tapping sound on the door captured my attention again. My brain, not yet fully awake, struggled to make my body leave Emmy's side, but I pulled on a pair of jeans and went to answer the door.

"Damn, I'm coming," I muttered, dragging a hand through my hair.

A hotel attendant greeted me then pushed a room service cart through the door and into the living room. "Just sign here, please." He thrust a slip of paper at me.

"I'm sorry, but I don't recall ordering anything." We'd

116

stayed up most of the night talking and having sex, so my head was a little fuzzy this morning, but I didn't recall phoning for room service.

"No, you didn't." He pointed to the paper. "It was ordered by a Miss Fiona Stone. All paid for."

I signed the receipt and handed it back to him. "Thanks," I mumbled and watched, confused, as he slipped out the door.

Emmy came padding out of the bedroom a moment later, dressed only in a tank top and a pair of my boxer briefs. I took a moment to just take her in. Slender legs, curvy hips, full breasts, and hair tangled and loose around her shoulders. *Mine*.

"C'mere, baby."

She crossed the room on bare feet and wrapped her arms around my waist, nestling in against my chest.

I pulled her close, relishing the feel of her small, soft body pressed against my firm one. "You stole my underwear," I whispered into her hair.

"Sorry, did you want them back?" she said sweetly, that little southern twang in her voice just barely evident.

I tilted my head down and stole a look. "No, they look better on you." My hands slid from her waist to her ass, cupping it in my palms and squeezing gently. I felt my girl shiver lightly. "You fill out the back nicely," I murmured near her ear.

She giggled and it was the sweetest sound, light and carefree. "Yes, but you fill out the front in a way I never will."

"I sure as fuck hope you never do. I don't think I'd like you with a dick, baby."

She laughed again. "What's all this?" she asked, motioning to the service cart.

"Uh, breakfast, I suppose."

"How thoughtful." She kissed my mouth before stepping out of my arms. "I just want to grab my laptop and see if I can connect to the Wi-Fi before we eat."

I nodded and watched her bend over to retrieve her laptop bag. Her ass looked good enough to fuck. She cleared her throat and my eyes darted up to hers.

"How about you pour me some coffee while I fire this up? There is coffee, right?"

"Uh . . ." I quickly scanned the cart and found a silver carafe of what I presumed was coffee. "Yeah." I poured two mugs of coffee, added milk, and set them on the round dining table. I made myself busy while Emmy powered on her computer. I transferred the dishes, silverware, and helpings of the food to the table. I poured us each a glass of what appeared to be pineapple juice. "Is it working, babe?" I asked over my shoulder. I knew she was taking her new assistant job seriously. I found her work ethic sexy, though of course I wouldn't have minded in the least if she treated this trip like a vacation and lay on the beach the entire week. She deserved a break after all the shit I'd put her through recently.

"Yep. I've got a signal. And it looks like Fiona sent an email with the details for the shoot tomorrow. It begins on the beach at nine a.m. There's an attached page of grooming instructions."

"Yeah? What's it say?"

She chuckled under her breath. "Wow. There's an astounding amount of detail on the way your pubic hair should be trimmed. Basically short . . . oh my goodness. Is this serious?" She let out a short laugh.

Honestly, it wasn't that surprising. I often received specific instructions for shaving my face, chest, and abs. This was a little out of the ordinary but not that unexpected. It was a swimsuit shoot, after all.

"What else does it say?" I asked.

Her eyes had gone wide and she sat silently blinking at the screen. "Fiona's left a note underneath the instructions." Her voice was shaky.

"Read it to me."

Emmy took a deep breath. "See you tomorrow, love. And P.S. I know these instructions won't pose a hardship for you, considering you've always kept yourself nice and neat. Love, Fiona."

Within seconds, I'd crossed the room and was guiding her away from the computer by the shoulders. "Ignore her. We both know that was a cheap attempt to get a rise out of you. My cock is yours. Just yours. Okay?"

She nodded, her eyes locked on mine.

I leaned in and kissed her softly. "Sit down, baby. Enjoy your coffee." I pushed the mug toward her and she lowered herself into the chair. "Eat up," I urged, sitting down across from her. "We have the whole day to play before work begins tomorrow." I wanted to get her mind off of Fiona's bitchy message.

"What are we going to do?"

"Anything you want. Snorkeling, scuba-diving, sunning ourselves, napping, hiking, oh, and apparently we need to shave my balls at some point too."

She giggled. "Ben!"

"What? I'm a rule follower, baby. And you're my assistant now, so I think you should have to help. Supervise, at least."

She shook her head, a pretty smile on her mouth. "Thank you for ordering breakfast. This is delicious." She nibbled on an apricot pastry drizzled in honey. Part of me wanted to keep quiet, to let her assume it was me, but an annoying voice in the back of my head pointed out that Fiona was likely to mention something about sending us breakfast. I needed to prove to Emmy that I could be honest about the big stuff as well as the little things.

"Actually, Fiona had it sent over," I murmured in between sips of coffee.

Emmy's eyebrows shot up and she dropped the half-eaten pastry to her plate as if suddenly losing her appetite. She roughly swallowed the bite she'd been chewing, the food visibly being forced down her throat. "Oh." She rose from the table. "I'm going to shower."

Shit.

Having lost my appetite as well, I called the concierge and requested that the food be removed right away so it'd be gone before Emmy was out of the shower.

I would have ordered her breakfast and fed it to her in bed

if Fiona hadn't interfered. Christ, what a mess being stuck between these two women.

When Emmy emerged from the bedroom dressed in a pair of cutoff jean shorts, red tank top, and tan sandals, it seemed her good mood was back. She looked adorable and sexy at the same time. A smile overtook my mouth. "C'mere, pretty."

She hesitated, blinking at me.

"Emmy." I held out my hand and she crossed the room and took it. "Are you okay?"

She nodded thoughtfully but didn't speak.

"Don't let her take this from us. I was so happy last night and this morning waking up with you." I brought her hand to my mouth and kissed her knuckles. "I'm yours, baby. Trust me, okay?"

She nodded again, blinking up at me with unshed tears. I cupped her jaw and angled my mouth to hers. I felt her arms wind around my waist. We fit perfectly together. I just needed to keep reminding her of that. And the only way I seemed to know how to do it was with physical affection. I wasn't good at pretty words. I was better at fucking and dirty talk.

"As pretty as you look in these little shorts," my hands slid down the sides of her thighs, "I need these and your panties off."

Her eyes darted up to mine and she dragged her tongue across her top lip. "I thought we were going out." Her voice was quiet, timid. I had to show her that she was mine. Desire flared up inside me and I answered it the only way I could.

"Let me fuck you," I whispered near her ear and felt her shudder.

I quieted her fears about us, about Fiona, the best way I knew how, by clearing her head of all thoughts but one—getting me inside her. I wasn't sure why, but I loved to hear her beg for my cock to fill her. Watching her come undone was the best fucking sight in the world. And the way she fit around me like a glove was unreal.

When I started pushing her shorts and panties down her hips, Emmy was already squirming for my touch, already making those tiny whimpering noises that I loved.

Emmy

We'd had two rather unproductive days on the island so far, preferring to remain locked away in our room making love rather than facing the world. We'd christened every room in the suite, having loud, sweaty sex. Part of me wanted to stop him, to tell him that he couldn't chase away our difficulties with sex. Yet, of course, I hadn't. I'd let him take me. I was too greedy for his touch.

But this morning we were both up and getting ready for Ben's first photo shoot in Fiji. I gulped down the remainder of my coffee and checked the clock. We had to be down to the beach in twenty minutes. I wanted to get there early to check on everything, though I supposed worrying about the set details was no longer my concern. My only job now was to make sure Ben arrived on time.

I grabbed my camera and packed it into my oversized purse. I planned to take a few behind-the-scenes photos today and post them to Ben's various social media sites for his fans to enjoy. A pang of sadness welled up inside me at the thought. Millions of women admired this man. Would he ever really be mine?

Dating someone in the public eye was all new for me. Ben had graced the covers of men's magazines, billboards, and advertisements around the globe. People worldwide had seen his provocative ads, women everywhere had fantasized about this man. And now he was choosing me. It was a lot to take in.

But I was a firsthand witness to the man himself, the actual person behind the glossy magazine pages. I'd seen him at his best, his worst; knew about his many prescription medications, his long-standing affair with his agent. He was known the world over for his physical beauty and stunning physique, but I knew what was in his heart, in his mind. Loving him provoked an achy intensity inside me. I wanted to soothe him, and hide him away from the world. But it was now my job to help promote him.

Realizing we had only fifteen minutes left to go, I pushed away the thoughts. Crossing the room, I tapped on the bathroom door and pushed it open. "Ben?"

"Almost done, babe." He shut off the water and stepped out of the shower, reaching for a towel.

"Holy crap," I muttered, pressing a hand over my mouth.

"What?" His gaze followed my line of vision south, and he smirked.

He'd shaved.

Everything.

"Nothing," I murmured. "You just . . . um, look a lot bigger."

His thick cock hung flaccid down his thigh. And as I watched it, it began to rise.

"Ben! We don't have time for that. We have to go."

He chuckled, the rich sound rumbling from his chest. "Then stop looking at my dick and telling me it's big, sweetheart. Guys tend to like that." He wrapped the towel around his hips and secured it into place. "You can play with him later, I promise."

"Just hurry up, I don't like being late." I strode from the bathroom and left him alone.

Lord, that man had an insatiable sexual appetite. I was fucked. Literally.

When we finally made it down to the beach, Fiona was chatting with the photographer, Gentry. A girl was sitting in a makeup chair with her back to me while a makeup artist worked on her. Ben's coworker today, obviously.

When she turned I instantly recognized her. London. One of Ben's former girlfriends I'd met last summer in Paris. I hadn't known that she'd be here. She was clad in a barely-there fire-engine red string bikini so small I could see her ovaries.

When she hopped down from the chair my breathing faltered. She was perfectly tanned and toned with bouncy curls and smoky eye makeup. She looked stunning. A slow smile curled on Fiona's lips as she watched me look over London.

My heart throbbed in my chest as I watched Ben warmly greet London. *Why hadn't he told me his ex would be here?* She pointed at the assortment of briefs he'd be expected to wear and they shared a laugh.

Ben approached Gentry next and shook his hand. They talked for a few minutes then he disappeared inside the on-site trailer to change into his first swimsuit.

I stood there, uselessly digging my toes into the sand, feeling utterly alone and out of place without his presence. There was no way I was talking to Fiona and I was too shy to approach London. I doubted she'd remember me from our one awkward encounter during the industry party in Paris. That was the first night Ben informed me, and the world, that I was his girlfriend.

Several minutes later the door to the trailer opened and Ben stepped out.

Holy Speedo, Batman.

His abs and chest looked amazing but when my gaze traveled lower to the large bulge protruding proudly in his snug briefs, I nearly choked on my own tongue. God, he was delicious. All hardened muscle and masculine beauty wrapped up in one tempting package. I wanted to throw a towel around him and shield him from view. Obviously a ridiculous notion considering what he did for a living.

Ben padded barefoot over to the makeup artist, who mussed up his hair so it was perfectly rumpled and then dotted concealer on a few spots before rubbing down his naked skin with bronzing lotion. I wondered if that lotion was edible because he looked good enough to lick.

They got into position and began shooting, several poses

together lounging in the sand and playing in the surf, and then changed swimsuits, repeating the process.

I normally loved watching Ben work, but watching him cuddle in the sand with London, wrapped up in each other's arms and frolicking in the waves, was not fun. Not one bit. I hated seeing Ben's perfect hands, his long fingers, gripping London's trim waist. I hated the familiar way her hand curled around his bicep. My stomach twisted like someone had twirled a fork inside me. I felt sick watching them.

They looked great together. The perfect couple. Just knowing they'd been a real couple, that they'd been intimate, that London was one of the three girls Ben had slept with killed me. Deep-seated fear and insecurity rushed up inside me, clouding my head, and making me question everything.

Needing a minute to myself, I turned my back on the shoot and walked off down the beach. I gulped lungfuls of fresh ocean air, pushing away the urge to cry. It was stupid. Ben loved me. He'd told me that repeatedly. But there was no denying that watching him pose, hold, and caress his ex on set was hard. I wasn't that secure in our relationship to begin with. And London, well . . . she was a perfect ten. Winner of the genetic lottery. And she'd slept with my boyfriend. *Awesome.*

When I made it back to the set everyone was packing up. Ben and London sat at the edge of the water, butts planted in the sand and feet out in the lapping waves. Ben tipped his head back, obviously amused at something she'd said. Taking a deep, calming breath, I boldly approached them. Ben rose to his feet, pulling me into a hug.

"Baby, there you are. Everything okay?" His hazel gaze probed mine.

"Fine," I lied.

London stood, dusting the sand from her petite bottom. "Hi, Emmy!"

"Hi." Gosh, she was gorgeous and nice too.

"That outfit fits you perfectly, I'm glad to see." She smiled at me.

My brow creased as I struggled to understand her meaning. Ben shifted uncomfortably next to me.

London tipped her head back, laughing. "Ben called and asked for my help shopping for you. I picked out all your vacation clothes." She smiled at me again, her bright white teeth gleaming in the sunlight.

My stomach dropped like a stone. I thought Ben had picked out and packed the pretty clothes for me. Learning that it was actually his ex-girlfriend stung like a venomous bite. "Oh. I hadn't realized. Thank you," I managed to choke out. "Yes, the clothes fit." No doubt several sizes bigger than London herself wore. Lord, that was embarrassing. The diet started tomorrow. I would wake up early and run every morning, not eat carbs, or anything processed . . . I began dictating the diet plan in my head when Ben's arm slipped around my waist and tugged me closer.

"Talk to me. You seem upset."

My gaze traveled to London and she returned my uneasy expression.

"Hey." She placed a hand on my shoulder. "Ben and I dated several years ago. It was short-lived and"—*sorry*, she mouthed to Ben—"not all that meaningful. We've both moved on. And I've never seen him happier. I'm happy for you both."

"Thank you." I nodded. It was stupid and insecure of me to feel threatened by their friendship. I repeated that over and over in my head. I didn't want to be that type of girlfriend. But my damn heart was still throbbing painfully in my chest as I watched London walk away.

Ben was still planted firmly in the sand at my side, waiting for my response. I swallowed heavily. "I feel so in the dark all the time with you, Ben. You should have told me that London was going to be here."

His eyebrows lifted. "I swore I told you she was booked for this shoot with me."

I shook my head. That was not a detail I'd forget.

He pressed his forehead to mine. "I'm sorry, sweetheart. I was so preoccupied with actually getting you to come, I didn't think. And I wanted your bags all packed and ready so that something so mundane didn't stand in your way. I called London and gave her my American Express. I knew she'd know just what to do. She dropped off all the bags at my apartment and I looked through every article, imagining you in them, and packed them all in the suitcase myself."

I smiled at his soft, tender tone, the look of genuine concern for me in his eyes. He was trying. He might not know the first thing about being a boyfriend, but he was trying.

"I love you, baby. Please don't invent things to worry about. There's nothing between London and I. We're friends. I promise you."

I flinched ever so slightly. He'd promised me things before. And now Fiona was pregnant and the last three women he'd slept with all stood within thirty feet of each other on this sandy beach. "I'm sorry." I shook my head to clear the thoughts running rampant. "I must be getting a little emotional."

He took my hands in his. "Don't apologize for how you feel. When I saw you take off down the beach it took everything in me not to go after you. I want to know how you're feeling, what you're thinking. Always. But promise me you won't take off again."

"I promise," I murmured.

Ben tipped my chin up to his. "Breathe for me, Emmy."

I pulled in a deep, shuddering breath.

"There, that's my girl." His hands moved up and down my bare arms, lightly caressing them. He caught something in my tone. "Now tell me what else is bothering you."

"I just didn't know London, um, bought my clothes," I murmured.

"No, baby. I bought them. She picked them out."

I nodded. I knew that.

"Now tell me what this is really about." His tone was sure and steady.

"This world is all new to me still. When I saw your hands all over her, the way you two looked together . . . I just started ticking off all the ways I don't measure up."

An angry wave of tension rolled off him and his hands curled around my elbows, locking me in place and pinning me with his eyes. "I'm thankful as shit you don't fit into this world. You remind me that there's so much more to life. You're my something real to grasp on to at the end of the day. You ground me. I love you and that's not going to change just because I spent the day rolling around in the sand with London for my job."

My gaze drifted downward.

"Baby." He lifted my chin again. "It might look glamorous, but my sand-chafed balls would disagree."

I chuckled lightly. "I think I'm ready to go back to the room."

He nodded. "Then let's go. I need to wash all this damn bronzer off my skin, too."

We'd just started back for the hotel when Fiona stepped in our path, her happy little smile pinning Ben. "I wanted to say thank-you," she purred.

"Uh . . . okay," Ben said, eyeing her curiously.

"For the baby shower gift. That was very sweet of you, love," Fiona said, addressing Ben.

He'd gotten her a baby gift?

My body went rigid and I felt Ben's hand tighten around mine. So much for the promise I'd just made not to run. I felt like fleeing for the moon right about now. Forget that, the moon wasn't far enough.

"You're welcome," he retuned, his tone short but polite.

Fiona sauntered away, her hand resting against her ever-growing belly.

Ben gripped my shoulders, turning me to face him, his face stricken with panic. "I want you to know, I didn't get her something for her baby. I just chipped in ten bucks toward the office gift. It was a stroller from everyone at Status; it wasn't just from me."

"Oh." I shouldn't care, should I? She was still his agent. He worked for Status. That meant he was practically required to chip in on the boss's gift. He was looking at me with the most worried stare. I took a deep breath and released it slowly. I placed my palm on his cheek. "It's okay. I'm not mad. She tried to make it sound worse than it was—but that's to be expected. She's a bitch."

A crooked smile overtook his mouth. "So you're not mad?"

"I would have preferred if you didn't chip in at all so she wouldn't have anything to grasp on to, but it's fine."

He kissed my lips. "You're the best. I don't deserve you and I know that. I handed Gunnar the ten dollars without even thinking. I'll try to be more aware of this type of thing."

I hoped his love would be enough to outweigh all the baggage threatening to overwhelm me at every turn.

Ben

The cool blast of air-conditioning inside our room felt terrific. Emmy kicked off her sandals at the door and sunk to the couch. I leaned over the back of the sofa and kissed the top of her head. "I'm going to shower." I wasn't kidding about having sand in some pretty undesirable locations.

"Okay." Her tone was despondent. But reading her subtle signals, and desire to be alone right now, I left her and closed the bathroom door behind me.

Stepping under the spray of hot water, I stood there uselessly, letting it beat down against my back, easing out the tension in my shoulders. I wish I could make Emmy see what she meant to me, help her understand that I wasn't this way with other women. Ever. She was special, everything I'd ever wanted.

I didn't hear the bathroom door open, but sensing I was no longer alone I opened my eyes and found Emmy's big, grayish-blue gaze watching me.

"You need a hand?" Her gaze slid down my naked chest

and abs, darting back up just as quickly. Her breath shuddered in a soft inhale.

"If you think you can handle the job." My voice dropped low and my face stayed impassive.

Emmy's tongue wet her bottom lip and her nipples pressed against the little cotton camisole she wore. As if taking a moment to think it over, she paused at the threshold to the marble-and-glass–enclosed shower. I remained still, standing in the spray of warm water. All except for my cock, which started to slowly rise in his own salute.

Apparently done thinking, Emmy pulled her shirt over her head and stepped out of her shorts. It took her just a moment to unsnap her bra and kick off her panties and then she was stepping forward, reaching for my outstretched hand.

Knowing the tumultuous start to our trip, I wasn't about to push her for more right now. But I'd also never deny an opportunity to be close to her, skin to skin. I pulled her to my chest and held her, letting the water soothe us both.

"Did you wash the sand off?" she whispered, standing before me.

"Not yet. I was just enjoying the water." It took every ounce of control I possessed not to bring my hands up and cup her breasts, rake my thumbs across her perky nipples. I loved the seductive look in her eyes when I took over. But I needed to be in control right now. Everything but my cock had gotten that memo. He was still steadily rising and was brushing past Emmy's thigh.

She swallowed heavily. "Let me wash you."

I nodded.

Emmy grabbed a thick washcloth from the shelf mounted to the wall just outside the shower. She wetted it and squirted a generous amount of body wash before lathering the suds. "Turn around," she commanded, looking determined.

"Yes ma'am." I turned away and she began scrubbing my back with a firm pressure. I let my head drop forward. Fuck, that felt good.

She continued soaping me up, not missing a square inch as she ordered me to turn and face her then raise my arms. I chuckled as she scrubbed my underarms then dropped them to my sides while she focused on soaping up my chest.

Her touch was so careful, so loving, it stole my breath and left me flooded with emotions I'd never had and couldn't name. I'd never felt so thoroughly loved and cherished like I did with her. She was the most selfless, sweetest person I knew. Real and true to her core. She wasn't the type of girl you dated and messed around with for fun. She was a forever type of girl. And the problem was, I wasn't a forever type of guy. I didn't know if I was even capable of that level of commitment. She deserved more. And the thought of hurting this beautiful girl and wounding her spirit wasn't something I ever wanted to do.

She ran the soapy washcloth along my arms and legs before wringing it out and depositing it on the bench seat in the shower. Then she dumped some of the liquid body wash into her palm and began rubbing it over my chest and abs. Her lips were parted and her hair hung in damp strands around her face, sticking to her neck. It took all the willpower I had to stand there and let her wash me.

Emmy's gaze slipped downward and her hands stopped on my hips. "You're getting hard," she murmured.

I looked down to where all her attention was captured. "Quite an accurate observation." I wanted to take myself in my hand, stroke and tease her, but I remained planted to the shower floor while rivulets of hot soapy water streamed down the length of me.

With a determined look in her eyes, Emmy brought her hands down to my length and gripped me lightly.

Watching her little hands try to stroke me was a beautiful sight. Her fingers slid from root to tip. "Fuck, baby . . ." I brought one hand to the wall, flattening my palm against the tile. "That feels so good." My voice was a deep rasp in my chest. Blood surged south as I pushed my hips forward to meet her hand's pumping.

She was still biting that damn bottom lip and watching me with wide eyes. I couldn't let my seed go to waste on the bottom of the shower floor. I wanted to be inside her. Done watching her play, I spun her around to face the wall.

"Hands up," I whispered near her ear.

She pressed her hands flush against the wall in front of her.

"Good girl," I murmured.

I stepped closer, pushing my body against the length of hers, loving the feel of my cock against the soft curve of her ass. I pushed her wet hair over her shoulder, leaning forward to tenderly kiss along the back of her neck and down her spine. I felt her shudder and her body broke out in chill bumps despite the warm water streaming over us both.

I trailed my fingertips down her spine, feeling her shiver and squirm as she anticipated where my hand was heading. Curving my hand between her legs, I found her already slippery and wet. I pushed my middle finger inside of her.

Emmy arched her back, forcing her ass back against me.

"Does that feel good, baby?" I dragged my finger slowly in and out of her.

Her low whimper and the flood of wetness I felt was the answer I needed.

I gripped her ass in my palms, spreading her cheeks and stepped closer, nestling my cock flush with her core. "This ass is so fucking sexy, baby." I gently squeezed and Emmy let out a soft groan. "You want me inside you?"

"Bennn . . ."

Hearing my name fall from her mouth excited me. And she seemed to use it often, addressing me in that sexy, unsure way she had.

I pushed forward, the head of my cock disappearing into her tight pink opening. "Ah, fuck," I groaned as I watched myself slip inch by inch deeper inside her.

Emmy pushed her ass out, her hips grinding back against my slow thrusts.

My hands planted themselves on her hips. "Slow down, angel. I don't want to come yet."

Snaking one hand around her front, I found her sensitive

nub, and though I knew from her frantic, jerky movements that she wanted me to touch her there, I took my time, circling the tender spot to draw out her pleasure. Emmy groaned, her hand closing around my wrist to keep my hand where she wanted it, and my dick went even harder, if that was possible.

Increasing my pace, I pumped my hips against her, pounding into her until I was fully buried. Little gasps escaped her lips as she rested her cheek against the cool tile.

Finally I flicked my fingertips over her clit and her hips bucked forward, working against my hand. "That feel good, honey?"

"Yeah," she breathed.

"This pussy's mine, baby."

"Yours," she moaned.

I circled her clit faster until uninhibited moans were tumbling from her mouth, as if her body were an instrument designed for my pleasure. I felt her pussy clamp down around me as her orgasm hit.

"Bennn . . ." she groaned long and low in her husky voice.

"Baby. Ah, fuck . . ." Her body went limp after she came and I wrapped my arms around her waist, pulling her body up and down on my cock a final few times. Biting into the soft skin on her shoulder, I came in long spurts deep inside her.

Later, once we'd fed each other dinner in bed and were wrapped up snuggly under the sheets, I caressed Emmy's back, lulling her to sleep.

"Baby?"

"Mmm," she groaned sleepily.

"About tomorrow's shoot…" I hesitated. Her eyes blinked open and found mine. "The photographer mentioned wanting to get some topless shots of London tomorrow. Nothing too revealing—hands and limbs would be strategically placed, but still, I wanted to warn you. You might not like what you see."

"Oh." She was quiet, but all her attention was trained on me.

"So I had an idea I wanted to run by you."

"Okay."

I brought my palm to her cheek and lightly stroked her smooth skin. "I've called and scheduled you for a session at the hotel's spa tomorrow. But only if that's something you want. Otherwise, of course you can come to the shoot. I have nothing to hide. I just want you to be comfortable."

She thought it over for a minute. "As your assistant, I should be there," she said, finally.

I took her hand, lightly stroking her knuckles with my thumb. "Yes, but as my girlfriend, I want to make sure you can handle it." There was more … but I didn't want to upset her. Deciding on complete honesty, I continued, "The set assistant today made some comment about not bringing significant others to the shoot."

"Oh." She stiffened. I knew we were both remembering how she'd stormed off across the sand once I'd started shooting with London.

I stroked her hand. "You didn't do anything wrong. I

should have prepared you better." Which was true. Swimsuit shoots tended to be sexier, and this one happened to be with my ex. I wasn't thinking. It was a dickhead move.

Her eyes lifted to mine. "Actually the spa sounds lovely."

"Good." I pressed a soft kiss to her mouth. "Your appointment is at ten."

"Thank you," she whispered and then curled herself into my body.

11

Emmy

I entered Nirvana spa with ten minutes to spare and was greeted by the soothing sounds of steel drums and ocean waves pulsing low through the speakers.

I approached the reception desk and was greeted by a young woman. "Welcome to Nirvana."

That had quite a ring to it. I gave her my name and she flipped a page in her notebook—no computer system here—and tapped her finger against the paper. "Yes, you're starting with a hair and scalp massage, followed by a warm seashell full-body massage, then a sugar glow, banana leaf wrap, exfoliating facial, waxing, and then manicure and pedicure."

Wow. Ben had really gone all out. Booked everything on their spa menu by the sounds of it. I nodded as a slow smile uncurled on my lips.

I was led into a small, dim room with a massage bed in

the center. The soothing music was playing in here, too, and I was instructed to remove everything but my underpants and slip under the crisp, white sheet. I did as I was told as soon as she was out of the room, already anticipating the experience.

When the door reopened, an older lady who couldn't have been much over five feet tall entered and greeted me with a warm smile.

"Welcome. My name is Elenoa. Are you ready to begin?" She had a pretty Polynesian accent, her voice gentle with almost a singsong quality to it.

"Yes, very much."

She graced me with another warm smile. "You're really getting the full package today."

That was Ben, treating me to the very best . . . unless he thought I needed all these treatments to look better. No. I wouldn't let my ugly insecurities mar this day. He was being generous. Nothing else.

Elenoa turned to the small counter and began mixing various ingredients into a small wooden bowl. "We've cultivated a unique blend of pressed nut oils infused with tropical flowers that rejuvenate and nourish your skin. Today I'll use a mixture of passionflower, white ginger lily, and virgin coconut oil."

I nodded. That sounded lovely.

She set to work and the relaxing blend of aromatherapy oils, coupled with the expert way her hands kneaded my stiff muscles, sent my mind wandering in a relaxed, dreamy state.

I thought about my parents back home and felt a twinge of guilt. My parents had been married for twenty-five years and had never had a vacation. Not even a honeymoon. Suddenly all this felt far too extravagant. But my mom had been happy for me when I'd called and told her about the trip. I shouldn't feel guilty. I should enjoy this. We were here for Ben's job.

Being Ben's assistant certainly had its perks. My tension-free body and semiconscious mind were proof of that. He was a great boss. I wondered what he was doing right now. Probably frolicking on the beach with London and her coconuts. Even though I was thoroughly enjoying all these luxurious treatments, I vowed to myself that next time I wouldn't abandon Ben alone at a shoot. Elenoa scrubbed my entire body with a ginger root masque then wrapped me in warm banana leaves, which felt so warm and good. I felt like a yummy, fruit concoction. If I reached out and licked my arm, it'd probably taste good. While the warm body masque set, I was treated to a papaya fruit enzyme facial.

After all the body treatments were done, the painful part began. She said the couple days' worth of stubble on my legs was the perfect length for waxing, and so I got full legs and a Brazilian bikini wax. I was pretty confident the latter hurt worse than childbirth, but the result was so pretty and smooth. After a manicure and pedicure I headed back to our hotel room. Ben was still gone so I ordered us lunch from room service and fell back onto the bed to rest. Was this really my life? Because a girl could get used to this.

I squirmed on the bed, trying to get farther away from Ben's reach. When he'd returned we'd eaten lunch, showered, and crawled into bed, still naked and damp, to cuddle.

"Don't." I tugged the sheet up higher around my waist to shield my lady parts, never mind the fact my breasts were bare.

"Let me see." Ben smiled, his eyes playful on mine. He'd seemed amused when we showered, wanting to look at the Brazilian bikini wax that left me completely smooth and bare. "I need to inspect their work. Make sure you got the full-service package." He gripped the sheet and tugged it away as I opened my hands, letting it slip down. Ben's gaze left mine and traveled slowly downward.

I pushed my thighs together. "Stop looking at it. It's awkward."

Ben pressed my knees apart. "Look at yourself, baby. You're beautiful." His fingertip lightly stroked my inner thigh and little chill bumps erupted along my skin. "Has no one ever told you how pretty your pussy is?"

My cheeks erupted in heat. I shook my head. Sex in the dark, under the covers, was my norm before he came along.

"It's like a little pink flower . . . look." I dared a glance downward. His thumbs parted my inner lips, the gentle touch both highly erotic and innocent. A throaty breath escaped me and Ben's gaze found mine. "See, you're perfect down there."

"If you say so," I murmured.

"Don't you like looking at me?"

I nodded eagerly.

A slow smile crept over his mouth. "Good to know. Well, that's how I feel about looking at you. You turn me on so much, baby."

Glancing down, it was impossible not to notice the rather large bulge at his hips where the sheet tented outward.

It didn't seem to be possible for us to go more than a few hours without sex. I kept waiting for that part of our relationship to cool, but that hadn't happened yet. He was sexy as hell and my body craved him. I wasn't about to deny it.

12

Emmy

I woke to Ben trailing soft sucking kisses against the back of my neck. I was still fitted against him, just how we'd curled up the night before, cradled in his arms. Except now the evidence of his arousal was pressing against me. It was hard to miss a nine-inch cock nestled against the seam of my ass. I pressed back against him, eliciting a low moan. "Baby, you can't do that." His tone was a warning, his voice deep and sleepy. Ben laid several more damp kisses along the side of my throat as I turned my head, my mouth seeking his. I squirmed against him, rocking my hips and dragging my backside over his cock. "Fuck," he murmured. "Misbehaving early this morning, Miss Clarke."

"I think you secretly like it," I taunted, rolling toward his scent and his gravelly voice. He was so incredibly sexy that I couldn't resist the temptation of his body primed and ready so close to mine.

We lay side by side and one of his large palms cupped my cheek while his other hand moved between us, feeling me as though testing how wet I was.

"Shit, baby. You're soaked."

Blood rushed to my cheeks. I dipped my head, but eyes leaving his, suddenly feeling self-conscious about my body's overly obvious reactions to him.

"Hey. I love that. It's a big fucking turn-on." He pressed one long finger into me and I let out a needy whimper.

"Do you need to come?"

"Bennn . . ." I rocked my hips closer.

"Shh. I'll make it better." Ben lifted me from the bed, momentarily stopping his delicious torture to remove the T-shirt I wore.

His fingertips traced the curves of my breasts, while his other palm lightly cupped my other breast. His touches were so soft, so careful, I could tell he was holding back. He was trying not to rush me, take me hard like he did up against the shower wall two nights ago. His hands trembled ever so slightly and I could feel how badly he wanted me. It was intoxicating. His thumbs brushed against my nipples and they tightened against his touch.

Pressing damp kisses to my throat, his tongue darted out to press against the spot in my neck where my pulse was thrumming wildly. He worked his way lower, licking and nibbling on my nipples. His fingers lightly curled around my ribs, holding me close.

His tongue lightly traced around my nipple, sending sharp darts of pleasure to my core. His teeth grazed my hardened nub and I felt the sensation deep inside my body as my sex clenched. My heartbeat pumped violently in my chest.

Situating me across his lap so I was straddling him, he pushed his boxer briefs down low on his hips and stroked himself twice. "You ready for me, babe?"

Locking my gaze on his, I drew a shuddering breath. I had him at my disposal day and night, and it still wasn't enough. The more I got of him, the more I craved of him. The deeper I began to understand him, the more I wanted to know. The closer we got physically, the more of myself I wanted to give to him.

Positioning himself against me, Ben pushed inside me, his big cock stretching me and stealing my breath from this angle. Sensations burst inside me and my head dropped back, exposing my neck to his kisses.

"Fuck, you're so perfect," he growled against my skin. I could do little more than hang on to his shoulders while Ben pumped into me. "Hold on tight." I wrapped my arms around his neck and clung to him. Ben's hands moved under my ass and pushed me up and down harder on him. The pleasure built inside me with each stroke, and after a few more blissful moments I came, clawing his back and digging my heels into the bed as I moved against him.

His fingers dug into the soft flesh of my hips and he clung to me, burying himself fully within me as he came.

We collapsed together back on the bed, each of our hearts pounding and both of us breathing audibly in the otherwise silent room. I didn't know how it was possible but every time with him seemed to get better and better.

After he'd cleaned us up and dressed me once again in my T-shirt, I tugged him back to the bed to lay with me again. I wasn't quite ready to get up for the day yet. He pressed his face into the crook of my neck.

"I like this spot," he mumbled against my skin.

He could stay there forever for all I cared.

Turning to face me, Ben tucked a strand of loose hair behind my ear. His expression was watchful, almost concerned, like he had something on his mind.

Ben

She was gorgeous like this. Unaware of her own beauty, her skin glowing and pink from her orgasm. I tucked a lock of hair behind her ear and she let out a soft, contented sigh. "I want to take you somewhere, be alone with you for a few days."

"Okay." Her eyes danced on mine.

"Great, because I've chartered a plane to fly us to a neighboring island. We'll spend the rest of our trip at an exclusive resort on a private island. Just us."

Her mouth blossomed into a wide grin, and I could read her expression as plain as day. No Fiona. No photographer. No ex-girlfriends to distract us. We'd be utterly alone. "What about work?" she asked. "Will there be an Internet connection so I can at least check on upcoming jobs for you?"

"No need to work. I've already let Fiona know I was taking you away. With the holidays coming up, this also tends to be my slow time of year anyway. It'll just be another week. Ten days tops." I grinned.

"I'd love to stay. I'll just have to let Ellie know I won't be home."

I pressed a kiss to her mouth. "Good. Let's have brunch; I'll have the hotel staff pack our bags. Our flight leaves in an hour."

"Wow. Honestly, I can pack my own bag."

"You're awfully bossy for an assistant. Come on. I'm hungry. And I'm craving those mango pancakes they have downstairs."

She chuckled and flung the blankets from her legs. "Fine. Let's feed you."

That was my girl. The food pusher I knew and loved. She couldn't resist the opportunity to take care of me or feed me, and I loved that about her.

13

Emmy

After brunch we spotted Fiona on our way to the car. The bellhop following us with bags in tow caught her attention. "Headed out?" she asked, stopping in front of Ben.

"Yes, I emailed you," he said. "I'm taking Emmy away for a private getaway before we head home."

I braced myself, watching her reaction.

A fake smile tugged at her mouth. "Okay, love. Go enjoy yourself now before the baby comes. You deserve it. Things are about to get busy." She laughed and hugged Ben, pressing her baby bump into his abs.

Ben said nothing to disagree; he just nodded and brought one hand around her back and gave it a careful pat.

I wanted him to claw her eyes out, not comfort her.

An acidic taste filled my mouth at the thought of him

leaning over Fiona's hospital bed to coo over her gorgeous little baby, inspecting it for signs that it looked like him.

He's promised me he didn't want her—that we'd still be together no matter what happened with the baby. But I wondered if that'd change once he saw her mothering his child. And if he had no interest in her romantically, could I handle him playing the doting dad to her baby. God, I sounded selfish. I was jealous of a baby. How pathetic was I?

I dragged my sorry ass behind Ben to the waiting car.

After the brief plane ride on what I learned was an *island jumper*, we were shuttled by a sedan to a private thatched hut, not a hotel. I spun around to face Ben.

"Are you serious?" I grinned.

"I only want the best for my baby."

I leapt into his arms, tackle-hugging him.

This place was paradise. Secluded and romantic. I doubted I'd ever want to leave.

The bellhop left us and our suitcases alone in the hut with just the gentle sound of lapping waves to accompany us. There was a large bed in the center of the room dressed in white fluffy bedding, two bedside tables, and a sofa across the room. Very simple, yet beautiful and elegant. I wandered toward the door leading out from the far end of the space with Ben trailing at my heels.

The bathroom vanity and a small room for the toilet were inside, but the shower itself was outside. Gray slate stones stacked more than chest high provided some privacy from the beach beyond, and a waterfall-style showerhead hung from the center of the ceiling.

It was absolute heaven. With the gentle lull of turquoise waters lapping the shore and a steady ocean breeze to keep the hut comfortable, it was everything I imagined a South Pacific paradise would be.

During the trip, it was as though we were both trying extra hard to be the perfect couple, to not let Fiona's warning haunt us or mark our time together. For ten days, we lounged in hammocks on the beach and sunned ourselves until we were a deep golden brown, despite our best efforts at slathering on sunblock. We swam, ate entirely too much, and sipped cocktails in the late-afternoon sun. There was no phone, no TV, no Internet. Just us. As much as I tried to ignore it, I couldn't help but feel like a clock was ticking, marking down our time together. I wondered if Ben felt the same way. He was extra sweet and attentive.

My monthly cycle made an appearance, so I spent the entire week bloated and fighting off chocolate cravings. Ben was amazing, though, massaging my lower back, ordering dessert even when I insisted I didn't need it, letting me sleep in, and generally being the world's most responsive boyfriend.

Most mornings after waking late and eating a light breakfast in our room, we walked straight out the front door and onto the sand to wade into the warm seawater for a morning swim. But this morning, Ben turned toward me, smoothed the hair back from my face, and watched me as though mesmerized.

He looked at me like something big was on his mind, but for the time being he remained silent, just stroking my cheek, running his fingers through my hair and watching me.

"Did you sleep okay?" I asked, finally.

Ben

Emmy watched me curiously as I ran my fingers through her long, silky hair. "Did you sleep okay?" she asked finally.

"Fine." I nodded. The truth was I hadn't slept for shit last night. I laid awake thinking about the very real possibility that Fiona's baby was mine. Could I really turn my back on her and the child? Growing up without a father figure, I'd vowed that I'd never be a deadbeat dad. And the more time I spent with Emmy, the more I began to worry about how close we were growing. Thoughts of Fiona and the baby weighed heavily on my mind. Somehow seeing her rounded belly this week made it all the more real. There was no denying she was getting bigger all the time. There really was a baby growing in there.

"Is something wrong?" Emmy asked, her forehead creasing as she watched me.

I didn't answer for several long moments and Emmy pressed her palm to my cheek. "Everything's fine," I managed. "It's probably time we got back to reality."

"I suppose we should." She rolled closer and stretched. "This has been perfect." She rubbed her hands over my bare chest, absently, as though her body dictated that we be touching anytime we could. "It'll be almost Thanksgiving by the time we get home."

"I suppose it will." It was almost Thanksgiving, though you wouldn't know it from the balmy eighty-degree days we'd grown used to in Fiji.

"What are you doing for Thanksgiving?" she asked.

"Ah . . . nothing, most likely. Last year my housekeeper, Magda, brought me some leftovers. The year before that I was in Brazil for a shoot."

"So you won't be with your mom in Australia?"

"Nah. Probably not. We haven't discussed anything. And they don't celebrate American Thanksgiving in Australia. Are you planning to go to Tennessee?"

"Yes. Would you . . . want to come home with me?" I could read the indecision in her eyes. I wondered if she worried it was too soon to bring me home, or if she worried that her parents wouldn't like me.

"If you want me there, of course I will."

Her eyes brightened. "You could meet my family, see where I come from."

"I'd love that." I lifted her hand to my mouth and pressed a kiss to her knuckles. Everything about my relationship with Emmy was uncharted territory for me, but I didn't mind. I guess we'd find out if I was good with parents. It wasn't her mom I was worried about—I was pretty sure I could win her over. It was her father who had me nervous. And it was the South. Didn't they shoot first and ask questions later?

14

Ben

I'd always known Emmy had grown up differently from me, but this wasn't what I had imagined. I pulled the rental car into the gravel driveway that Emmy pointed out and cut the ignition. Her parents lived in a rust-colored old trailer with a crooked front door and a bare patch of dirt where the grass had been trampled away over the years.

I glanced over at Emmy. She chewed nervously at her lip, watching for my reaction.

I grabbed her hand, lacing my fingers between hers. "Ready, babe?"

She gave a tight nod and climbed from the car.

Gravel crunching under my boots, I followed her lead to the front door. She hadn't told me much about her parents, only that her mom and dad and younger brother would all be here for Thanksgiving. I hadn't really had the typical experience of meeting my girlfriend's parents before, so I wasn't sure what to expect. The door opened when we got closer and Emmy's mom came barreling out to launch herself into Emmy's arms. They were sobbing and hugging and talking in animated voices while I stood there uselessly holding Emmy's suitcase and my duffel bag.

She hugged her dad next then leapt into her brother's arms, calling him "Bubba!" He shook his head and her mom leaned over to explain it'd been her nickname for him since he was born. She'd been two years old and couldn't say Porter.

Her mom had long brown hair like Emmy's, with a few threads of silver in the braid hanging down her back. As soon as she released Emmy and wiped stray tears from her cheeks, she turned to face me. I couldn't imagine such an emotional homecoming with my own mother. The last time I went to visit her two years ago she couldn't even be bothered to come and pick me up from the airport. She sent a driver, with the excuse that she had a manicure appointment to keep.

"Heaven above, Emerson Jean. He's hotter than the month of July."

"Mom," Emmy scolded, turning pink as her mom looked me up and down. "This is my mom, Sue."

"Hi, Mrs. Clarke." Before I had time to decide between a handshake and a hug, she was launching herself toward me. Twining her arms around my waist, she gripped me in a hug as I patted her back under the watchful scowls of Emmy's father and brother.

Clearing my throat, Sue finally released me and stepped back. I crossed the weathered front porch and extended my hand. "Mr. Clarke, it's nice to meet you. Thank you for having me."

Never in my life had I felt so scrutinized, even when strutting down the runway dressed in next to nothing. I felt the intensity of the glares served up by the men in Emmy's life.

Emmy stepped in between us. "This is my dad, Tom, and my brother, Porter." They continued glaring at me. "Dad," she hissed, and her father slowly raised his hand to shake mine.

"Welcome to Tennessee."

The relaxed smile that overtook Emmy's mouth told me she'd been more worried than she'd let on about her father's reaction to me. Her brother was still watching me with a frown etched into his face. Porter was about my height and spent more than his fair share of time in a weight room. Judging by his tense posture and expression, he was considering challenging me to a wrestling match out in the front yard.

A huge black dog came barreling out the front door and charged straight for me. His snout hit me squarely in the nuts. "Ompf." I doubled over as the breath was forced from my lungs.

"Buck!" Emmy yanked him back by the collar, successfully dislodging the beast from between my legs.

I looked up to see Porter smiling for the first time. "Good boy, Buck."

Emmy elbowed her brother in the ribs.

"What? He's just being protective, Em."

"It's fine," I bit out. My voice was several octaves too high and my balls were aching but I took the hit like a man.

I straightened and felt my balls descend back to their proper place. Fuck, that hurt.

"Come inside, Ben," Sue said. "I can get you something for your . . ." Her eyes darted down to my crotch.

Emmy let out a groan.

"I'm fine. Thank you, though."

Sue placed her hand in the crook of my arm and led me inside. "It's not much, but it's home."

The inside of the trailer was cramped and dim and the floor groaned under my feet, but it seemed comfortable and homey. "It was very kind of you to invite me." I let her guide me to the little front room that held a matching sofa and love-seat in baby-blue corduroy fabric. It didn't escape my notice that I had to pass by the well-stocked gun cabinet on my way to the sofa. I was sure Tom designed it that way.

I sat in the center of the smaller sofa, Emmy on one side and Buck hopping up to sit on the other. He sat there like a damn grown man, looking down at me. It was clear I was going to have to work to win over the Clarke men. Dog included.

Her mom handed us glasses of sweet tea and sat down across from me and Emmy. "So tell us about yourself, Ben. Or is it Benjamin?"

"Ben's fine. And what would you like to know?"

Porter settled onto the sofa next to his mom and Tom sunk into a worn armchair across from the television.

"Well, Emmy tells us you're a model," her mom offered.

Tom rolled his eyes and stifled a groan. It wasn't a profession he respected. At least not for the man dating his daughter.

"Yeah. I've been modeling since I was seventeen. I enjoy it. I get to travel all over the world and meet lots of interesting people. It's actually how I met Emmy."

Her mom smiled, seemingly pleased. After a few minutes of idle chatter, Sue said, "Emmy, why don't you put the bags in your bedroom? You'll sleep in your old room and Ben can bunk with Porter, or sleep out here on the couch."

"Couch should be fine, right champ?" Porter said.

"Yeah, sure thing." I hadn't realized I wouldn't be sleeping with Emmy. She gave me a sympathetic look that said she knew all along. I'd wanted to book a hotel for us but the nearest one was fifteen miles away and Emmy had said her parents would be offended if we didn't stay with them.

Seconds later, Emmy was pulled into the kitchen to help bake pies and I was left sitting there with a dog that looked ready to attack me and two men watching me like I was some sort of dangerous and unpredictable species. I glanced at the shotgun mounted on the wall in the dining room. Yeah, I was fucked.

Actually I wasn't, considering I wouldn't be sharing a bed with Emmy. Not that I would have fucked her under her father's roof anyway, but a little messing around would have been nice. I couldn't resist making Emmy come. Her cheeks flushed so pretty and those breathy little whimpers she made were so sexy.

Shit. I couldn't be thinking about that right now. Not while Emmy's dad looked ready to skin me alive.

Emmy emerged from the kitchen with a pink frilly apron

tied around her middle and her hair twisted up in a bun. With hands covered in flour, she leaned down to press a kiss to my cheek. "You okay hanging out with the guys, hon?"

I chuckled hearing her southern accent becoming more pronounced being near her chatty mom. "I'm fine. Go enjoy yourself." She clearly loved being home. I hadn't seen her smile so bright before.

"Well, should we do it?" Tom asked, rubbing his palms together.

I looked from him to Porter, trying to understand what he intended. It was tempting to watch the sway of Emmy's ass as she sauntered back into the kitchen but I kept focused. The man already hated me.

"We're going out hunting. Got to get us a turkey for tomorrow."

Shit. This should be interesting.

Emmy

Ben looked stunned to hear that he'd be going hunting with my dad and brother but he rose from the couch, seemingly game for an adventure.

My mom stomped out from the kitchen, appraising Ben's designer chinos and button-down shirt. "Your clothes are much too nice for romping around in the fields. Emmy, go get him a pair of your dad's britches."

Oh. My. God. My mom was officially insane. Did she really think Ben would be comfortable wearing a pair of my dad's old Wranglers? I wanted to die. Seriously, I closed my eyes and silently prayed that the floor in the trailer would miraculously cave in and swallow me whole.

"I'm fine, Mrs. Clarke. Thank you, though," Ben said, politely refusing her request.

I watched Ben leave with the men in Porter's old pickup truck and a wave of nerves hit me. I wondered how he'd fare alone with my dad and brother. But my mom thrust a ten-pound bag of potatoes at me, and I knew peeling them with the old, dull knife from her ancient knife block would be the perfect distraction.

I knew my family life was much different from Ben's. I could only hope he'd fare okay with my dad and Porter. And hunting no less. There were firearms involved.

"So does Ben want marriage, kids? He's got a pretty non-traditional lifestyle, sweetie." My mom was nothing if not direct.

"Uh . . . I'm not really sure. We haven't talked about it." Other than my drunken rant telling him we'd make attractive kids. That was just a damn fact of life, though. Any babies with his DNA would be stunning specimens. Superior in every way, I was convinced. Little hazel-eyed babies with dark hair and full, pouty mouths danced through my head while I methodically peeled the potatoes.

My mom abandoned chopping a pile of onions and turned to face me. "How could you have not talked about it? You're dating pretty seriously. . . . You're not one to just bring home a man, Emerson Jean."

She was right, of course. I'd never brought home a man for a holiday like this before. And I did feel differently about Ben. I wanted him to be my future. I guess part of me was just scared about his possible baby with Fiona and their relationship, even if it was professional now. Mostly I worried that he couldn't possibly want the simple life I'd envisioned for myself since I was a little girl. A home down the street from my parents, big family holidays, baking pies with my mom, and, one day, my little girl. The sour feeling in the pit of my stomach rolled with unease. "He didn't have anywhere to go for Thanksgiving. His mom lives all the way down in Australia. I didn't want him eating Chinese takeout."

Her look of concern told me I was probably crazy, reading way too much into our relationship.

An errant tear dropped from my eye.

"Are you okay?" she asked.

"Yeah, it's just those damn onions," I lied, gazing at the pile of chopped onions on the counter. The weight of her concerns about Ben burned like acid in my stomach. How had I allowed myself to fall for someone so wrong for me? The only reasoning I could find was that it was never a choice.

Loving Ben Shaw wasn't something I ever planned on doing. Lord knew my family and friends warned me from getting emotionally attached. But I had zero control in the matter.

I had two choices: to enjoy the ride for what it was worth and accept him and his limitations or move on without him.

It wasn't a choice. I wouldn't turn my back on him. My heart, my body, my entire being craved him like a drug.

Her expression softened. "I support you and whatever makes you happy. I just want to make sure you're being careful with your heart this time."

I tossed the potatoes into the pot with more force than necessary. "I've got it, Mom."

Of course she was only trying to help, and she'd seen me at my worst after my breakup with Ben obliterated my heart like it'd been through a blender.

"Well, is he religious, does he have the same values as our family, Emerson?"

Religious? I didn't think so. Not particularly. But he had values I respected. He was hardworking, willing to help out friends, dedicated, and faithful. That was all I needed. Of course now that my mom had mentioned it, I was dying with curiosity to know his stance on marriage and kids. Even getting him to say I love you seemed like a giant leap for him. I was just hoping no one grilled him over dinner on politics or religion. My damn family would scare him off before we even got started.

Somehow the awkward pauses and tense silences hanging around the men had evaporated by the time they returned from the annual turkey hunt. Porter dealt with the bird in the garage and my dad and Ben came inside, all smiles and loud stories. I bounded into the living room. How very homey . . . my man coming home with my daddy after hunting.

"Woman, I bring meat," Ben said with a chuckle, mimicking a deep, cavemanlike voice.

My dad laughed and patted him loudly on the back. "He did well. He's a great shot."

I beamed up at him, fighting the urge to kiss him silly. He'd never looked sexier—returning from a hunt with my father; the smell of fresh air, sweat, and male bonding. I could envision him being part of my family and that thought sent a little thrill racing through my system. Coupled with my mom's talk earlier about marriage and babies, my mind was on overload with visions of matrimonial bliss. I needed to stop. I was acting crazy. Lord, I could only imagine my mom's reaction if she knew about Fiona.

"Nice job, honey." I pressed a kiss to his throat and scurried off to the kitchen before I molested him in front of my dad. I couldn't imagine that'd go over well.

After eating an amazing home-cooked dinner of barbecued ribs, beans, and corn bread, we drank glasses of sweet tea. My dad even broke out his special aged whiskey reserved for special occasions to pour himself, Porter, and Ben glasses.

My dad stood at the head of the table and raised his glass. "I'd just like to properly welcome Ben here to Tennessee. Say thank you for bringing my girl home safe and sound."

The smile on Ben's face and the twinkle in his eye was priceless. I wanted to bottle that contented, happy look and save it to enjoy later. Seeing him around my family tonight, I was repeatedly hit with a pang of sadness that he didn't have this type of relationship with his mom, and to the best of my knowledge, didn't know who his dad was. I was glad to see my family welcoming him.

After dinner I helped my mom wash the dishes while Ben helped my dad clean the guns. Porter hadn't seemed to warm to Ben yet and took off for a local tavern for a beer by himself. Even though he was my younger brother, he acted like he was ten years older—always had. He was superprotective of me, so it didn't surprise me he hadn't taken to Ben just yet, although I hoped he would in time.

At bedtime my mom and I helped Ben cover the couch with sheets and left him extra blankets and pillows. I lingered beside the couch and Ben's dark eyes landed on mine. My mom cleared her throat. "Say goodnight, but nothing funny, you two. It would make your dad really uncomfortable."

"Of course, Mrs. Clarke. Thank you for your hospitality."

Ben had such good manners in front of my parents. I loved seeing this side of him. Knowing there was a filthy-talking sex god lurking just under the surface of this well-mannered man was a big turn-on. Huge.

My mom disappeared down the darkened hallway and only the low light from the television was left to illuminate us. It was the first time we'd been alone all day. I wanted to wrap my arms around his waist, bury my face against his neck, and breathe in. But I knew once I felt his firm body and inhaled his delicious scent, I'd want more.

His hand slid under my hair to cradle the back of my neck then he tilted my head and pressed his lips to mine. "Thanks for bringing me home," he whispered.

"Thank you for coming." I leaned my head back into his palm.

"I'm gonna win your dad over. You know that, right?"

I nodded, unable to take my eyes from his. "Are you going to be able to sleep?"

He gave my neck a gentle squeeze. "I'll be fine. You get some rest."

I scurried down the darkened hallway to my bedroom before I changed my mind and tackled him onto the couch.

After brushing my teeth and changing into sweatpants and a tank top, I crawled under the covers of my familiar old bed. Pulling my grandma's quilt up to my chin, I lay there wide-awake, wondering if it'd ever be possible for Ben to fit into this life.

I tossed and turned on the lumpy, narrow mattress until well past midnight. My mom's words rang in my head. Unanswered questions, topics Ben and I had never discussed. Not to mention he just looked out of place in this shabby trailer. Too commanding, too big, most assuredly too beautiful. It suddenly felt like a big fucking deal that I didn't know his stance on marriage and kids. I'd fallen hopelessly in love with him without even knowing if we were compatible, if we were building toward something real.

My heart raced in my chest. God, I felt like an idiot that I didn't have the slightest idea what his opinion was on these major life matters. These were nonnegotiable for me. My chest felt tight and achy. I couldn't go through another breakup with Ben. My heart wouldn't survive it. I felt like crying. I curled into a ball and hugged my pillow as silent tears streamed down my cheeks.

Damn it.

I wasn't going to get any sleep at this rate. And my eyes were going to be all puffy for Thanksgiving tomorrow. I threw back the covers and climbed out of bed. I'd get a glass of cool water, collect myself, and then get back in bed.

I crept down the hallway, navigating the worn pathway easily in the dark. I filled a glass with tap water and chugged it in the darkened kitchen before a noise from the living room caught my attention. Ben was stirring. Shit, maybe he'd never even fallen asleep.

"Emmy?" he whispered loudly. "Is that you?"

I rolled my eyes. He was going to wake everyone in the tiny trailer with his supposed whispering.

I put the glass in the sink and went to the living room. The soft glow of moonlight filtering through my mom's lace curtains illuminated him on the couch, rubbing a hand through his messy hair. "Come here," he whispered, softer this time. "I'm horny," he said as he chuckled softly.

I knew I should head back to my bed but I couldn't resist getting close to him. I sunk to the couch, curling into his side.

"Hey, what's wrong?" He pushed the hair back from my face, looking me over in the darkness.

I wiped my cheeks by instinct, though my tears were now dry. "I can't tell you."

"Of course you can. You can tell me anything."

"But . . ."

"Shh." His hand cupped my cheek. "I already know, Emmy." My eyes met his as his thumb soothed the skin along my jaw. "Our lives are different," he continued. "Me being here highlights that. But I told you I'm going to win over your dad. And actually, I enjoyed hunting today."

I nodded. "I know my parents like you already. That's not what this is about." God help me. Did I even have the courage to tell him the crazy thoughts running rampant in my mind?

"Emmy, breathe for me, baby."

I pulled in a deep, shuddering breath, my lungs tightening with the effort.

"Tell me." His tone was commanding but his gaze was worried and sincere.

"What's your stance on marriage?"

He coughed. "Marriage?"

"Yes."

"Ah, shit." He rubbed a hand through his rumpled hair. "It seems like a fine institution."

I was in too deep now. I decided to push on. "I mean, do you want to get married someday?"

"Is this your way of asking me where things are headed with us?"

"I guess so," I said, my voice a weak murmur.

"Hey, look at me." Ben lifted my chin until my eyes met his. "I want you. I want this. I've never had a serious girlfriend before, so I'm sorry if I've given you the impression I'm not committed to us—I am. And I know things with Fiona are fucked up . . . but don't question this."

I swallowed. "I'm not. I'm just scared. I see my life—my future—and I want kids, a devoted husband. I'd like to live here in Tennessee near my parents someday."

He swallowed, his Adam's apple bobbing visibly in the dim light. "I didn't have the best example growing up. My mom never married. I haven't really ever thought about it. Shit, I never thought I'd be in a serious relationship like this. Just give me time, okay?"

I closed my mouth, unwilling to press him further, and nodded. It wasn't the exact answer I'd been looking for, but it was all he had to give. His hand curled around my waist and he pulled me closer so that I was pressed against him on the couch. His hands rested on my hips, clutching me firmly to him, and everything felt right. He might not have given me an answer my mom would be happy with, but it was enough. For now. He was willing to try, for me.

My heart rate kicked up and suddenly my body wanted more. More everything. More contact. More him.

I didn't care that we were in my parents' living room. I needed him. Wanted to feel his skin against mine. Nothing else mattered.

I pulled my T-shirt over my head and dropped it to the floor. My bare nipples tightened in the cool night air.

"Holy shit. What are you doing?"

"Now I'm horny."

"Baby. I was kidding before. We can't. Your parents . . ."

"I need this. Please . . ."

"Fuck, baby. Don't tempt me. You know I want to make you come."

"Yes, please, Ben."

Ben

Hearing her beg for it was too much. I needed her. Needed to get her off. But, fuck, we were in her parents' living room. Anyone could get up for a glass of water or to use the bathroom, and then I'd be fucked. Likely with one of those impressive shotguns pointed in my face. But my daring side was willing to risk it.

I briefly considered taking her back to her bedroom, but seeing how that was right next to her parents' room, I wasn't sure that option was any better.

"Emmy, we can't," I protested weakly as she crawled into my lap to straddle me. She pushed her pelvis down, wiggling in my lap, and I instantly went hard.

Fuck it.

I knew she felt it too because she released a breath, squirming against the hard ridge in my shorts.

Shit. I wanted to fuck her. In her parents' house. This was bad. I couldn't let this happen. She was grinding against my dick. "Emmy, no."

I lifted her off me and set her on the sofa beside me.

Not wasting any time, she started untying the drawstring on my shorts. Instead of stopping her somehow, my hips lifted, allowing her to tug the shorts down my thighs. My dick sprang free, resting against my belly.

Emmy licked her lips then dropped down to her knees in front of me.

Fuuuck. The eager-to-please look in her eyes was so incredibly sexy. But seeing her on her knees in front of me was almost my undoing. I wanted nothing more than to feel her mouth around my dick and I wouldn't stop her now.

Emmy's soft hand closed around me, and my head dropped back against the sofa. She stroked me slowly from base to tip. My body reacted to the simple contact, fluid beading as she stroked me. I was powerless to stop it. Fuck it. I pushed my shorts to my ankles and brought a hand to the back of Emmy's head, guiding her mouth down to my needy cock.

I watched her lips close around me and I was lost. She might feign innocence, but shit, she was good at giving head.

Her mouth opened wider and her cheeks hollowed out as she sucked me deeper.

"Ah, shit, baby." I guided her, showing her I wanted it deep, and Emmy happily obliged, taking every inch.

She had the distinct ability to make me feel things I'd never felt before. It had never been just sex with her. She was pleasing me, taking care of me, putting my needs first. It overwhelmed me and a feeling of being loved settled over me.

I'd never wanted to label things, to plan out every last detail of my life, and just the words "holy matrimony" made my skin itch. It just wasn't in my DNA. But if anyone had the ability to change my mind, it'd be this girl. I couldn't let her leave me, which meant I might need to rethink my future of bouncing from city to city.

But for now, I focused on the beautiful girl on her knees in front of me, enjoying the mind-numbing bliss she was delivering. And Emmy, ever the devoted lover, gave an amazing performance, her hands stroking, her tongue lapping against me, and little groans escaping her throat as she got into it.

"Come here, beautiful." I lifted her under her arms, pulling her into my lap again, and lowered my head to taste her breasts. Thrusting her chest out, Emmy whimpered as my tongue flicked back and forth over each swollen nub. I covered her mouth with one hand and worked the other into the front of her sweatpants.

I was unaware of anything but her so the rattling noise across the room took me a few seconds too long to realize it was the front door opening.

Emmy

Ben's incredibly skilled mouth teased my breasts, and just as his long fingers were about to reach my sex he suddenly pulled away, tossing me off his lap and onto the cushion next to him.

What the?

I followed his worried stare across the room.

Shit!

Porter was home.

He stood facing the couch, an angry scowl stretched across his normally relaxed face. "Fuck! That's my sister, dude!" He took a threatening step closer.

Ben shot up from the couch, tugging his athletic shorts into place. "My bad, dude." He held his hands up in front of him, palms facing Porter.

The vein in Porter's neck was throbbing and his fists clenched at his sides.

Oh, God. This wasn't good.

I leapt up from the couch, pushing my palms against Porter's chest to get him to back off. "Porter, this was my fault. Ben said we couldn't." My brother's face twisted in revulsion as he realized that yes, his sister liked sex and even initiated it. Too bad. That was a damn fact of life. Hi, have you *seen* my boyfriend?

"Not cool, Emerson. Get your ass to bed. In your own room."

My cheeks heated and I nodded. Stealing one last glance at Ben, who was now smirking, I scurried off down the hall.

My father carried the massive golden-brown turkey to the table, setting it down with an expression of reverence. It didn't matter that we were dining in our dingy, old trailer; we had one another, and family meant everything.

Once the turkey was carved and plated and the side dishes were served up in heaping spoonfuls, my father said a blessing and we quickly dug in.

Mmmmm . . .

This was why I came home for Thanksgiving. Right here.

Ben wiped his mouth with his napkin and turned to my mom. "This is delicious, Mrs. Clarke."

My mom smiled widely. She enjoyed feeding people even more than I did. It ran in the family.

"Porter's thinking about joining the military," my dad announced. Of course I'd known this. My mom had called me in a panic, but we hadn't actually discussed it yet. My eyes went to Porter's and he gave me a weak smile. The pride in my father's expression was evident. I knew he was hoping Porter would find his way, do something with his life. In many ways, Porter had grown up a lot since I had left him. He was more than a head taller than me, with lots more muscle too, yet he was still stuck here, living at home, figuring out his path.

"I think that's terrific," Ben commented, addressing Porter. "Have you enlisted yet?"

Porter shook his head and set down his knife beside his plate. I knew no one wanted to mention the events that led to him considering joining the service. After high school he floundered a bit, going out too often, and went through about every girl in this town and the next while he waited for our sweet neighborhood girl, Eden, to grow up a bit and notice him. When that didn't happen, he'd gone on a bender and gotten arrested for drunk driving one night. My parents had recently given him an ultimatum: Grow up and do something with your life, or get out. We'd yet to see what he'd actually do.

"So, Ben, do you have other aspirations besides modeling?" my dad asked. I couldn't help but see the comparison being made in my dad's head. Porter was doing something admirable in serving his country, and Ben's job was all about glitz and glamour.

"Well, it's not a career that usually carries you through retirement," Ben said. "One of the things I'd like to do, with Emmy's help," his eyes found mine, "is to set up a charity to eventually run."

His desire to run a charity was news to me but I immediately liked the idea. Of course I would help him. I grinned widely and his mouth quirked up.

We ate until we were stuffed, and then somehow managed room for the pumpkin and apple pies my mom and I had baked.

Ben and my dad had seemed to really hit it off. After dinner they sat in the living room talking for hours, my dad pulling out his atlas so Ben could show him on the map exactly where he lived and I lived in the city. I knew my living so far away made my father nervous, but somehow seeing that I had a capable man in my life had brought my father around to the idea of Ben.

Soon it was time for us to leave to catch our flight back to New York, and through a tearful good-bye between me and my mom, Ben promised my mother he would bring me back for another visit soon.

15

Emmy

Back in New York, Ben and I huddled close as we left the airport. The temperature was in stark contrast to the mild autumn air back home. I pulled my navy pea coat around my chest and burrowed into the scarf looped around my neck.

Ben guided me toward the waiting black sedan at the curb.

Henry.

It was nice not having to hail a cab. Especially since I'd never mastered the talent, despite being a New Yorker now. At this rate I wouldn't have to. Being part of Ben's life was amazing. Chauffeured car service, flying first class to cities around the globe, room service, and plenty of sex. I had a feeling once reality set in with dirty dishes, piles of laundry, and all the other annoyances of real life, I'd be in for a rude awakening. But for now I was living the dream.

Ben's knuckles rapped against the trunk as Henry popped it open and hopped out of the car to assist. I slid into the backseat and let them fight over putting the bags in the back. A quick glance in the rearview mirror told me Ben won, maneuvering both our bags inside and refusing Henry's help. We hadn't discussed where we were heading but I gave Henry my address and then dared a glance at Ben. His face was impassive. Good. At least I wasn't being scolded for wanting to go home.

We drove along the Grand Central Parkway, the sun glistening off the river below and warming my cheeks. Even if New York didn't quite feel like home, it was nice to be back. I'd been living out of a suitcase for far too long between Fiji and Tennessee. Plus I missed Ellie. I missed her like crazy.

As we stopped in front of my building, Ben exited the car to retrieve my suitcase, and to my surprise, guided me up the stairs. "Are you staying?" I asked. I figured he'd be as eager to get home as I was.

"For a bit, if that's okay. There's something we need to discuss."

I nodded and rescued my keys from the bottom of my purse before letting us inside.

Ellie was sprawled across the couch, blankets strewn around her prone body and a tub of ice cream sitting on her chest. "Argh . . ." She pulled the spoon from her mouth and sat up abruptly.

"Hi." I waved. Damn, I really needed to learn to give her a warning knock or something. She looked like hell. Baggy, stained sweatshirt and hair in a messy bun. "Everything okay?" I asked. It wasn't even noon and she was hitting the peanut butter fudge ice cream pretty hard.

"Men fucking suck," she announced.

"All of them or someone in particular?"

She rolled her eyes. "I'm going to my room."

Okay then. I'd talk to her once Ben was gone, figure out what in the world had happened. She hadn't been dating anyone when we'd left for Fiji.

Ben carried my suitcase into my bedroom and I trailed behind him. After depositing the bag on the floor at the end of my bed, he turned to face me. "There's something we need to discuss." He ran a hand down my spine, stopping at my hip to pull me close. He bent down to brush his mouth against the side of my head.

Flutters of heat shot up my spine, coloring my neck. "What?"

"There's something I want," he continued.

I'd give him anything. But the intense stare he was directing my way was intimidating. "W-What do you want?"

"Move in with me."

Whoa. What? I thought we'd covered this. "Ben."

"I hate when I have to take you home and leave you behind. I want you with me every night. I want to wake up with you every morning."

"Be serious. We haven't been dating very long."

"I am being serious, Emmy. Why not?"

He didn't know all my disgusting habits. And I didn't

want to know his. I needed my own space, my own bathroom time, for heaven's sake. "Don't you want your space?"

He stepped closer, his eyes locking on mine. "No. I want you in my space. You're mine. I hate the thought of leaving you here."

"You just need a warm body next to you to sleep."

His mouth twitched in a smile. "There is that. But not just any warm body." His hands curled around my waist. "This body." Sliding his hands lower, he caressed my hips lightly. "This tempting, sexy body," he whispered near my ear, sending chill bumps racing down my spine. "Plus we should live together for a while before we make things official, right?"

Did he mean . . . ? No, I couldn't be distracted right now, though. I had to tend to Ellie. I'd been a horrible roommate and a worse friend the past several weeks. Removing his hands from sinking any lower, I took a step back. My head was a mess. He was standing in my tiny bedroom telling me he was committed to this—to us—and wanted to share an address with me. "I need to talk to Ellie. Can I call you later?"

His mouth tightened into a line and his eyes settled on mine. *Shit*. He'd been vulnerable with me, opened up and explained his need to keep me close and his fear of rejection. And here I was, ready to reject his proposal. I took his hand in mine and squeezed. "Actually, I could come over later if you like. I just need to make sure Ellie's okay."

His mouth relaxed and he leaned down to kiss my forehead. "I'll send Henry back in a few hours."

"Okay." I wondered if I'd ever ride the subway again. Not

if Ben had his way. I'd be chauffeured around the city like a kept woman. But I'd address that later. I didn't want to refuse his generosity. We did, however, need to have a talk about boundaries and maintaining my freedoms at some point soon.

After seeing Ben out and locking the door at his insistence, I sought out Ellie, tapping lightly on her bedroom door. "Ells?"

"Yeah?" Her voice was rough. Agitated.

"Can I come in?" I peeked my head inside. She was curled up under a mound of blankets, staring blanking at her little TV in the corner. "Ellie? Are you okay?"

"Just fucking lovely." Her tone was laced with sarcasm. "Not to be a bitch, but the last thing I need right now is to be around two people in love."

"What happened?"

"Men happened. I'm done with them. I'm done with their bullshit excuses, their selfishness, waiting for them to call. I don't need them. I have two perfectly wonderful, functioning vibrators and I'll be taking care of myself from now on, thank you very much."

"Oh . . . kay." I wasn't sure what had brought this on. The last I knew she was single and wasn't really dating. "Did you go out with someone new?"

"Doesn't matter." She waved a dismissive hand. "Already forgotten."

"He didn't call, did he?"

"Nope. That asshat."

"I'm sorry, baby. I'll get the vodka."

"Thanks, pookie." She smiled at me weakly.

I loved how simple things were with Ellie. She was tough and smart and independent, yet in a lot of ways still needed someone to rely on. Deep in my heart I wanted to consider Ben's invitation to move in with him but I'd feel terrible leaving her—and now certainly wasn't the time to bring it up.

When I returned to her bedroom with two vodka–cranberry juice cocktails, Ellie was at least sitting up in her bed this time. She happily accepted her drink and took a long sip.

"Do you want to talk about it?" I asked, sipping my own drink.

"Not at all. Now, tell me . . . are you moving in with him or what?" she asked.

"I, um, I don't know. He wants me to, I just don't know if I'm ready."

She nodded, watching me with soulful eyes. "You know I love having you here, but don't let me stop you. You're stuck with me no matter where you live."

I smiled at her. "True." Our friendship wasn't defined by my address. "I think I'm just scared of jumping into his world so completely."

She nodded. "Then take your time and think about it."

"I will." The thing about Ben that she didn't understand was his need for love and acceptance. He'd grown up without love from two parents, any siblings, or a happy family unit. His mom was in and out of rehab and he never knew his father. He'd come to terms with all that, but I could tell the idea of me rejecting him scared him. And this was a guy who wasn't easily fazed in any other area of his life. The knotted tension in his shoulders, the intensity in his eyes when he'd asked me to move . . . waiting to see what I'd do, how I'd react. If I'd accept him. Him and all his baggage. And there was a damn truckload of baggage where that man was concerned. It was daunting at times. But still so easy to love him at others.

After cooking dinner with Ellie and making sure she was settled for the night, I was chauffeured back to Ben's place.

His lips at my throat greeted me. "Thanks for coming." I felt him inhale the scent of my neck and a shiver raced down my spine, igniting all my senses.

I nodded and lifted on my toes to press a kiss to his full mouth.

He had the lighting turned low, and the city lights that glittered through the large picture windows provided a pretty ambience. A bottle of red wine rested on the coffee table with two wineglasses and a fire crackled in the fireplace. *Wow*. It was very romantic and the perfect end to my day.

"Would you like some wine?"

I nodded and let his fingers dancing at my lower back guide me into the living room. We settled on the sofa and Ben offered me a glass of ruby-colored wine. Hazel and luminous green eyes roamed mine while I took a sip. Delicious. Flavors of spicy pepper and robust black cherry burst on my palate. It was pleasantly tart with just a hint of sweetness. Yum.

"Good?" he asked, trying his own.

"Orgasmic." I smiled.

Ben chuckled. "Not yet, lovely, but that could be arranged."

The promise of his skilled hands and glorious mouth on my skin later sent a rush of endorphins through my system.

Now that we were back in New York I felt hopeful that Ben and I could work out the differences in what we each saw for our futures. And hearing his comment about making it official put a kernel of hope in my heart that wasn't there before. Of course I didn't want to bring that up straightaway. We'd had too many heavy conversations lately, and an evening relaxing alone together was not something I wanted to spoil.

Ben lifted my feet onto his lap and pulled the throw blanket from a trunk beside the couch to cover us both. He removed my socks, dropping them beside the couch, and began massaging my feet. His thumbs rubbed along the length of my instep and I relaxed into his soothing touch, believing everything would be okay.

The feeling was short-lived, though, because moments later his phone began ringing from inside the kitchen. The first two times he ignored it, but the third time he lifted my feet from his lap and stood.

He cursed loudly, retreating down the hall with his phone in hand.

I heard his bedroom door close softly and the hushed sounds of his voice.

Tossing aside the blanket, I padded down the hallway to investigate. My scalp tingled and the hair on my nape rose. He was acting strange, secretive, and all my senses were heightened. I felt like an intruder watching my life unfold. I felt oddly disconnected standing there, heart pounding in my chest, fists clenched tightly at my sides, trying to eavesdrop. I fought to quiet my labored breathing so I could hear.

"One second. I need to check with Emmy," I heard him say from behind the closed door. The sound of my name snapped me back into the present.

"How bad is it?" he asked.

I wondered if it was related to his mother and her struggles to stay sober, and my heart ached for him.

"Because I do, Fiona. I won't cut Emmy out of this."

My stomach leapt into my throat. He'd gone behind closed doors to take Fiona's call privately.

The door opened and Ben stood there, clutching his cell phone in his hand. "Which hospital?" he barked into the phone, then he nodded once and ended the call.

What in the hell was going on? "Is everything okay?"

"No." His voice was flat.

"Was that Fiona?"

"Yes."

I waited, barely breathing, for him to explain what was happening. The vein in his neck was throbbing. He was angry, but about what, I had no idea. "Ben?" I dared at last.

"Fiona's been admitted to the hospital for exhaustion and dehydration. She's gone into early labor and the doctors are trying to stop it."

She was only about six months along. Way too early for the baby to come.

"Fuck." Angry hands tore through his hair. "I have to go."

I shot him a glare that questioned his sanity. "You're going? Now?"

"This could be my baby. I have to be there, Emerson."

An acidic taste rose up my throat. His baby? I hated the sound of that. Almost as much as I hated the sound of my full name falling from his mouth with such venom. I thought, if anything, he merely regarded himself as a sperm donor. The worry in his eyes and his haunted look told me he wasn't so sure. My heart throbbed painfully at this new realization. If the baby was his, would he want to be involved in its life? In Fiona's life? Could I handle him being linked to her for the rest of our lives? Would we spend birthdays and holidays together?

Gulping lungfuls of fresh air, I fought off the impending panic attack threatening to take me under. I couldn't handle a life like that. It might be selfish but I wanted Ben to myself. His profession dictated I was required to share parts of him I'd much rather not. I wouldn't share his time, too. I wouldn't split him with an evil witch like her. And I wouldn't watch him walk out the door to be by her side tonight.

"I'll go," I rasped, fighting to get my thumping heart to slow down.

He cocked his head to the side, one dark eyebrow rising. "Are you sure?"

I straightened my spine. "Yes. Absolutely." Better me than him. I could have a talk with her, woman to woman. Tell her to back the fuck off Ben. Roughing her up was out of the question in her fragile state, but I wasn't above telling her off.

"I don't know if that's a good idea. Are you sure you want to be alone with her? I could come along," he offered.

I shook my head. "I'm positive. I need to do this." I didn't want him anywhere near her. I needed to do this for me—to stand up for myself and for Ben. It was long overdue.

He didn't argue, and without further hesitation, I stuffed my feet back into my socks and shoes and shrugged into my coat.

"She's at Northwest Memorial," he said, staring down at his feet before meeting my eyes again with a pained expression. "Emmy . . ."

"Don't speak," I warned, pushing my palm between us.

He nodded. "One thing," he whispered.

I expected an *I love you*. Perhaps a *Be safe*, or a *Thank you for going*.

"Will you call me with any updates?" he asked.

I nodded and left. With no kiss good-bye, and no loving words exchanged between us, I fled into the night.

When I arrived at the hospital and asked for Fiona Stone, I was directed to the maternity wing on the fifth floor. Walking by the babies in the nursery window made everything more real. The soft coos, the happy new parents, and sleep-weary nurses bustling past me were a wake-up call. This baby was coming. Whether Ben and I were ready or not, Fiona was going to be a mom.

I found her room, the door left partially opened, so I took a deep breath and entered. Fiona was sitting on the bed in a turquoise-and-cream silk robe, slipper-covered feet folded underneath her, sipping a Pellegrino and flipping through *Vogue* magazine.

What the hell?

She didn't look ill. In fact she looked phenomenal. She had a healthy glow to her skin, red lacquered nails, and her hair and makeup were styled perfectly.

"Fiona?" My voice cracked.

Her eyes lifted to mine and her mouth puckered in a frown. "Where's Ben?"

"He's not coming." I wanted to feel excited, proud of that fact, but watching her face fall, I only felt empty. This woman was in love with my boyfriend and there would be no happy ending.

"Why not?" her confident voice shook ever so slightly.

"I told him I'd check on you myself, and he stayed home." I didn't mention that he'd asked me to call him with news.

She swallowed, as if summoning her courage. "I get it. You're threatened. You made him stay behind and came yourself so he wouldn't have to."

I peered down at the shiny tile floor. She wasn't far off from the truth. I didn't want to feel threatened by her, yet I did.

"He sent me, Fiona. He didn't want to come."

She took a fortifying breath and met my eyes. "You're nothing like the girls he has dated in the past. You know that, yes? I never thought I'd measure up to the models he attracted. London Burke . . . and many others. They were younger, thinner, prettier." She looked down, picking at an imaginary piece of lint on the blanket beside her. "But then you came along. I don't usually hire female assistants but I knew you'd pose no threat. From your dirty tennis shoes"—her eyes dropped to my feet—"to your ratty ponytail . . ." She clucked her tongue, her eyes pinning me in place.

She was doing her best to cut me open, but my tough outer shell remained intact. There was one key thing she didn't understand about Ben that I did. It wasn't what was on the outside that attracted him to me rather than her. She was a vindictive, manipulative witch. I was wholesome and loved him just for him. He got that. She clearly didn't. And I wouldn't be explaining that to her; I just stood my ground, keeping my face even and composed, doing my best to look bored by this whole exchange. She wasn't a threat. The baby might come between us eventually, but I was confident Fiona never would.

"Don't you worry about what will happen when we learn this baby is his?" Her hand went to her swollen bump, stroking it lovingly.

I didn't answer—couldn't. All the air was sucked from my lungs. I worried about that every waking moment. I had dreams of beautiful little babies that were a perfect mix of Fiona's dark, shiny hair and Ben's brilliant hazel eyes.

"I could get him back, you know. He's been with me for five years. He hardly dated. We traveled the world together.

Dined at five-star restaurants, made love in the finest hotels; I built him up to where he is today. Ben isn't the type to forget that. He's extremely loyal."

I forced air to return to my lungs and found my voice. "There's a good chance this baby isn't his. Do you really think he'll still be at your beck and call then?"

"That's what your poor, simple mind doesn't understand. I'm friends with his mother. I'm practically part of the family. I'll always be around."

At the mention of his mother and their ongoing relationship, something in me snapped. I was done being nice. I'd claw her eyes out if necessary and not think twice. "And if I called his mother and told her you seduced her son, took his virginity, how do you think she'd react?"

Fiona laughed maniacally. "I seduced him? If that's what he told you, he lied." A smug smile blossomed on her mouth. "Far from it, sweetheart. He wanted me. And trust me, I was all too happy to oblige. You two have been together what, eight months, nine?"

I nodded. She was keeping track.

"He and I have a history that spans five years. When you've made it that long, then you can talk to me about how well you know Ben. In the meantime, buzz off." She flicked her wrist in my direction.

"Why do you think I'm here tonight and he's not? He's not interested in you, Fiona," I enunciated each word slowly, letting them sink in. "Your attempts at winning him back . . ." I shook my head. "It's getting awkward. He's never been interested in more with you. You were convenient. A warm body while he was on the road. I'm the person he wants to build a life with."

Her smooth exterior began to crack ever so slightly. Her jaw twitched and tightened. "No. You think that, but I know him. He doesn't want to be tied down. Not with some no-body."

"Fiona, Ben's asked me to move in with him." My tone was direct, harsh, but it had to be to get through to her.

Her bottom lip trembled, the only indication that I'd finally succeeded.

"I'm not the enemy here," I continued, my tone softer this time. "You need to let him go. Even if the baby is his . . . he'll never be yours."

Striding from the room on shaky legs, I rounded the corner and stabbed the button for the elevator.

16
Ben

Emmy's brow was crinkled in deep concentration, her laptop balanced on her knees as she sat next to me on the sofa. I loved her work ethic and dedication to my career but I wouldn't have minded her taking a break now and again, either.

We'd been discussing options for my charity and whether it made more sense to start something of my own or join up with an established organization. We'd considered building orphanages for AIDS victims in Africa, setting up freshwater wells in Central America, and sponsoring early childhood education programs here in the United States.

"Thank you for staying over," I said, leaning down to breathe in against her neck. Emmy had been staying over more and more, and though she hadn't officially agreed to move in yet, she'd brought a duffel bag and left it in my closet. She knew I needed her here to sleep. Her toiletries and some spare clothes were inside, not yet unpacked, but I knew it was only a matter of time. A step this big should scare me, but instead it made me ridiculously fucking happy.

It was hard for me to admit it but I needed her. I'd never needed anyone, but this sweet southern girl was different. She had been from day one. Her refreshingly real attitude had knocked me on my ass—floored me right from the get-go.

I still remembered meeting her for the first time in Fiona's office and chuckled out loud.

"What?" Emmy asked, her eyes lighting up with a smile.

I knew she loved seeing me lighthearted like this. And early memories of her did that to me. "I was just thinking about the first time we met at the Status headquarters."

Her smile faded ever so slightly. "Oh, God." She buried her face in her hands. "When I spilled that tea all over the floor? I was a nervous wreck around you."

Interesting. At the time, I'd assumed it was just Fiona that made her so nervous and unsure.

"I can't even imagine what you must have thought of me," she continued.

"I thought you were stunning," I said, brushing the back of my knuckles along her cheekbone. "You didn't fit the mold of Fiona's typical assistant and I couldn't take my eyes off you. You looked so sweet and innocent. I wanted to corrupt you."

"I thought you barely noticed me," she said, glancing down.

"I noticed everything. How erratically your pulse fluttered in your neck when you looked directly at me." I trailed a fingertip down the column of her throat. "How your eyes peered straight into mine. I knew you saw the real me, and I was intrigued. But I also knew I should leave you alone. I knew Fiona wouldn't take the news well that I wanted to fuck her assistant."

Her quick inhalation of breath told me I'd hidden that fact well. That, or my choice of language surprised her.

"I thought you were out of my league," she admitted softly.

I laughed. "No. The other way around, sweetheart. You were real and genuine. I knew my mountains of baggage would likely scare you away. But everything in me wanted to devour you."

"I picked up on that once you started texting me." She smiled widely. "But I knew right from the beginning you'd be dangerous for me—that it wouldn't be just about sex. I knew I could fall hard for you."

"The feeling was mutual, trust me. Scared the shit out of me, too. I'd never needed anyone before. But after that first night we spent together you were a magic cure for my insomnia; I knew you were special. That you and I had something special."

Her little hand found mine and squeezed.

"And the fact that you cared enough to convince me to stop relying on those pills and always wanted to take care of me . . . I'd never been treated like that by a woman. Most were more concerned with getting my autograph, finding out if the shit they'd seen in the tabloids about my mother was true, or posing for a picture with me to post to their Instagram. It was all about saying they'd met me. You didn't care about any of that."

She met my eyes. "Not a bit. The nurturer in me just wanted to feed you."

I truly couldn't imagine my life without her in it. I'd never been one for commitment, but I needed to make sure she stuck by my side no matter what the future held. I couldn't fuck this up.

Emmy was in my bathroom drying her hair while I prepared a light breakfast of poached eggs and fruit for us. It turned out having her here made me want to cook. I transferred a bowl of blueberries and sliced pineapple to the breakfast bar just as my phone began to ring.

I padded into the living room and found it on the console table. *Damn.* It was Fiona.

"Hello?

"Hi, love," she cooed in her sharp British accent that I used to think was sexy.

"Did you need something?" The last thing I needed was Emmy finding me on the phone with Fiona, though I could still hear the blow-dryer running.

"Yes, I actually wanted to tell you that I've decided to go through with the paternity testing after all. It's driving me mad not knowing."

"Uh . . . okay. I'm happy to pay for it."

She huffed. "You know that's not why I'm telling you. I don't need your money, love."

No, I supposed she didn't. She had plenty of her own. She ran a top modeling agency in New York. She made 15 percent commission on everything I made, and I did quite well. "When will you know?"

"The test is on Tuesday, so about a week or ten days after that. I'll be sure to call you."

"Okay." I didn't quite know how I felt about all this. Emmy and I seemed strong right now . . . but if the baby turned out to be mine . . . I didn't know.

"Is Emmy there now?"

I could still hear the blow-dryer running. "Yes."

Fiona paused for a long moment, the sound of her breathing soft yet distinct. "Ben, does she know your past like I do? Does she know everything, including your little indiscretion from years ago?"

My mind reeled to follow her line of thinking. Then it came roaring back to me. My mistake two years ago. Of course I'd told Fiona about it at the time—as my manager it was possible she'd need to keep it from leaking to the public. I didn't know why she was bringing it up now, however. My stomach dropped. Unless she planned to use it against me with Emmy. "Don't fucking wreck this for me. I will walk away from your agency so fast."

"Ben, I'd never do anything to hurt you. You should know that. I'm just asking a simple question. Does she know?"

"No. And I hope she never will. Now drop it," I growled and hung up, resisting the urge to hurl my phone against the wall. Instead I let it fall from my open hand and onto the carpet with a soft thud. *Fuck.* I felt like punching something.

"Who was that?" Emmy asked, looking concerned and standing in the doorway.

I hadn't heard her there. "Ah. Nobody, baby." *Nice lie, asshole. God, what was wrong with me?* She frowned. "Come here." Emmy walked into my outstretched arms and laid her head against my chest. My heart was pounding like crazy. I couldn't have anything ruin us. "It was Fiona, actually."

"Oh?" She stepped back out of my arms.

"Yeah, she wanted to tell me she decided to have the paternity testing done after all."

"Okay." She visibly swallowed, her hands clenching at her sides. "So we'll know something soon."

"Yes, in one to two weeks."

Emmy took two more steps backward. "Why is she doing it now? She said . . ."

"I know."

Her arms crossed over her chest in a defensive stance. "If this is some angle to try and get you back. I mean, if you turn out to be the father . . ."

I tugged her close again, stroking her hair. "Hey, I'm not going anywhere. It's me and you, babe." I only hoped it stayed that way.

Watching Emmy move around my apartment, the striking force of realization that hit me was almost too much. I couldn't lose her. I knew with certainty I would marry her tomorrow if she'd have me; I'd move to Tennessee if that's what she wanted. Christ, it'd put us farther away from all the drama in my life and give us peace to just enjoy each other. I imagined us owning a country home that she could fill with beautiful things and delicious foods. I imagined watching her belly grow round with the life we created. It made me weak in the knees to realize how badly I needed something I didn't even know I wanted.

I felt something powerful surge in my chest. As soon as Fiona's test came back, I could have Emmy like I wanted. Like she wanted—marriage, a real commitment, a home we built together, and children in our future. Just us. No more drama. No more Fiona. I couldn't fucking wait.

"Shit, man, I never thought I'd see the day." Braydon shook his head, the beer bottle suspended halfway to his mouth all but forgotten. He stared at me, a look of surprise etched into his features, like I'd grown a second head. But I guess that's what happened when you told your best friend you were thinking of popping the question.

He was right, I'd never wanted to commit, never wanted to have someone in my life—until now. I used to love my life—coming and going as I pleased, jetting off to exotic cities, adding stamps to my passport, and not having to answer to anyone, except maybe Fiona. Now it all seemed so incredibly empty. And dull. And meaningless. I wanted more. And having Emmy by my side provided a certain comfort, a feeling of being loved and cared for that I had never known was missing. God, I sounded pathetic. If I actually said these things out loud, Braydon would probably tell me to grow a pair. And rightly so. I needed to have my man card checked. But shit, love made a person do crazy things. And I wanted to put a big old diamond on my baby's finger, see her eyes light up, and take her to the bedroom to make love to her slowly, to make her understand that she was mine forever.

He took a slug from his beer. "Ben mother-fuckin' Shaw settling down, committing to one woman, just one pussy to sink into for all of eternity. Damn, bro."

I shot him an angry scowl. His words were meant to scare me but they had the opposite effect. Knowing Emmy would be mine for the rest of forever sounded pretty fucking perfect to me. Although I hated knowing he'd been inside her, too. He knew just how perfect and sweet she was. The thought didn't sit well with me. I downed the shot of bourbon and held up the empty shot glass, signaling the bartender for another.

"Although it is Emmy. Shit, if she looked at me like she does you, I'd probably be getting down on one knee, too," Braydon said, looking contemplative.

"Yeah, right." We both knew Braydon preferred his single life way too much to make a commitment like that. His one serious girlfriend fucked him up pretty royally, too, so I didn't see him jumping on the relationship train anytime soon.

"Wipe that angry-ass look off your face. I'm happy for you, man."

"Thanks," I bit out.

"Can I be best man?"

"You promise not to talk about my future wife's pussy ever again?"

A lopsided grin lifted his mouth and he chewed on his lip as if deciding whether he could live with my request. I slugged his shoulder and the grin disappeared in a damn hurry. "Ouch. Fuck, man, you're touchy." He rubbed his shoulder. "She's all yours. You have nothing to worry about. That girl is crazy in love with you, too."

I smiled, knowing he was right. Emmy was perfect. And soon she would be mine. Forever.

It took me a moment to place the voice on the other end of the phone. Her broken sobs made it nearly impossible to make out what she was saying. "Fiona? Is that you?"

"Y-yes," she cried, heaving a breath inward.

"What happened? Is the baby okay?"

"Fine. The baby's fine." She quieted for a moment, seeming to pull herself together, because when she spoke again, her voice was much clearer. "The results came back."

My stomach sunk like a stone. "Okay . . . that's a good thing, right?" It was time to face the music.

"I suppose so."

"What's it say, Fiona?" I held my breath, waiting, while my heart jackhammered against my ribs.

"It's not yours, love." Her voice went whisper soft like she was breaking the news to me gently.

My fist pumped in the air, but I held back the shout of joy

I wanted to let rip. "Wow. So your last fertility treatment must have worked then?"

"Seems so," she said, her voice full of melancholy.

"How do you feel?"

"Shocked. Surprised. I really thought it was yours. And I'd gotten over thinking that you and I were going to be together, but I thought I'd always have this little piece of you. . . ."

We each remained quiet for a few moments, letting the weight of this information sink in.

"Fiona?"

"Yes, love?"

"I need to ask something of you."

"Anything."

"I need you to let me go, to release me from my contract early. I'm leaving Status to work for myself."

She hesitated briefly, releasing a heavy sigh. "If that's what you want."

"It is," I confirmed.

"Then I'll tear up the contract. Consider it my gift to you for five loyal years."

"Thank you." The tension in my entire body went lax at once.

"I'll always love you, Ben."

"I know."

"If anything ever changes between you and Emmy . . ."

"It won't. Good-bye Fiona."

"Bye," she murmured.

I wasn't going to be a father. A sense of relief washed over me. Fiona was out of my life and I was free.

I dialed Emmy the moment I pulled myself together.

"Baby!" I couldn't contain the excitement in my voice.

"Hi there. What's going on?" she chuckled softly at my enthusiasm.

"I have some news."

"Oh yeah? Everything okay?"

"Everything is better than okay. It's fan-fucking-tastic, actually."

She giggled. "Okay, so now I'm intrigued. What is it?"

"Two things actually." I knew I was drawing this out, torturing her, but Christ, we'd waited so long to hear this news, I didn't know how to just blurt it out. "I just talked to Fiona. I'm not the father."

Silence.

"Emmy? Did you hear me?"

"Yes," she whispered. I could imagine she was shaky and breathless, just like I'd been when I'd heard. "Oh my God, you don't know what a relief this is."

"Trust me, babe. I do."

"Ben . . ."

"I know, baby. I know. We can finally be together."

"I love you," she said. I could hear the smile in her voice.

"I love you more."

"Wait, you said you had something else to tell me."

"Yeah, I told Fiona that I was leaving Status. As of today, it's you and me, babe."

"That's wonderful, Ben. I'm proud of you."

Hearing her say those words meant everything. After all

I'd done to jeopardize things with her, apparently I was doing something right, too.

"I have news, too," she said, her voice teasing.

"Spill it, Tennessee."

"Guess what I'm doing right now?"

"What, baby?"

"Packing. I decided to move in."

Damn. This day was getting better and better. "You won't regret it. I'll be your love slave and take care of your every need."

"Hmm . . . I like that. Will you even go to the pharmacy and buy me tampons when I need them?"

If that's all it took to make her happy, I'd gladly do that and more. "You know it, baby."

I wished I'd been there to tell her in person, but she and Ellie were having a girls night tonight, and I wanted to be respectful of her time with her friend. "Can I take you out this weekend to celebrate?"

"That sounds perfect."

Emmy

My life had turned into a damn episode of *Maury*. But Fiona's plan backfired in the best way possible. Ben was not the father. After he'd called and told me, I'd collapsed into a heap on the floor, sucking in deep breaths like they were my first after being underwater too long. I hadn't realized how tense the whole situation had made me.

I felt as though a weight had been lifted from my shoulders, from our relationship, and it was terrific. And the happiness in Ben's voice was unmistakable, too. Thank God. Now we could finally move forward. And the icing on the cake was that he'd decided to separate from Status Models, from Fiona, and to work as a free agent. I would help him book jobs and he'd no longer be represented by her. He thought it was for the best, given all the drama over the past several months, and I couldn't agree more.

Everything was falling into place. I felt happy and secure with my job, our relationship, and even though I felt a little bad about moving out on Ellie, she understood and was happy for me.

Just as I was stuffing the last of my clothes into a suitcase, Ellie entered my bedroom. Her face was masked in a frown. I knew she'd been upset about guys lately, but I'd never seen her so down. "Ells?"

"Honey, you need to come here." Her tone was deadly serious and I wondered what in the world had happened as I followed her to the living room. She went to her laptop and began loading some type of video.

"What's this?" I asked completely dumbfounded about what we were doing watching some random video.

"You might want to sit down," she said.

I smiled uncertainly but lowered myself into a chair. "Ellie?"

Ellie pressed a button and the video began to play. My eyes struggled to comprehend the grainy images I was seeing.

I watched everything come into focus and . . . *Holy Fuck!* A naked couple was on the screen. He was going down on her and she was grinding against his face and moaning. The muscular back. His dark hair. There was something so familiar about it.

And then all at once I recognized him. Ben.

And the girl he was with was startlingly familiar, too.

Oh God. *London.*

He inserted two fingers inside her and she promptly came, calling out his name. He slid up her body and positioned himself at her entrance before pushing forward.

This wasn't happening. This wasn't real. No.

"It can't be," I whispered. He wouldn't. Would he? I leapt from my seat and began pacing the living room.

Ellie watched me with a worried stare.

Holy God. I felt like all the oxygen had been vacuumed from the room and my lungs were crying out for air. I curled my arms around my chest and sucked in a deep breath. Tears escaped from my eyes and rolled down my cheeks. No. God, no. This couldn't be recent. Could it?

"Emmy," Ellie caught me just as my legs gave out and guided me to the floor. I collapsed into a boneless heap, legs splayed and arms clutching myself as I slowly began to rock back and forth.

"No, no, nooo . . ." I muttered quietly, snapping my eyes shut. "Turn it off."

Ellie obeyed, leaving my side only briefly to click the pause button on her laptop.

It didn't matter, though. The images were burned into my retinas. There'd be no unseeing the way Ben's hips rocked into her, the way his fingers laced with hers above her head, a move he'd used on me, too. There'd be no unhearing the low growl in his throat when he entered her. Tears freely streamed down my cheeks and a silent sob broke from my chest.

Ellie sunk to the floor next to me and wrapped an arm around my shoulders. "I'm sorry. I just thought you needed to know."

"How did you find it?" I asked, through hiccupping tears.

"It's the top news story on every celebrity gossip site today."

I clutched my heart, gasping for air, and prayed it didn't give out on me completely. All the things we'd been through . . . every hurdle . . . now none of it mattered. Ben had betrayed me.

I realized Ellie was still talking about the video and I wiped away streams of tears and tried to focus on what she was saying.

"I don't know how it got leaked, or when it's from, but they're saying the girl in the video is his ex . . ."

"London. I know her," I croaked. "She was in Fiji with us . . ." An unwelcome thought slipped into my brain. Had he cheated on me when we were in Fiji?

"Yeah. London Burke. A model, apparently . . ." Ellie gave my shoulder a gentle squeeze. "Hey, you okay?" Her sympathetic look was too much. I saw in her eyes how foolish I'd been to trust Ben all these times. To give him all these second chances.

"No." Of course I wasn't okay. I doubted I'd ever be okay again. Ben had ruined me. Ruined me for all other men. For future trusting relationships. And my heart still yearned for him, stupidly enough.

"Vodka? Chocolate? A blowtorch to fry his balls? What do you need?"

"Nothing. I just don't want to be alone right now."

"You got it, babe."

I crawled from the living room floor onto my bed, sinking into the soft mattress. Somehow I was exhausted. Emotionally and mentally drained.

She pulled the blankets up around me and turned off the lights before crawling in beside me. Just having her weight on the mattress next to me was enough to make me not feel so alone.

"Maybe it wasn't even him, sweetie. I mean, it looked like him, but you never know . . ." Ellie said, softly rubbing my back.

"It was him." I knew it with absolute certainty. I recognized everything about the possessive way he fucked, the way his body moved, his measured strokes, the strong muscles in his back. There was no trying to pretend it wasn't him. "She called out his name, Ellie. It was him."

God, the whole world had seen my boyfriend naked and in all his glory. Or was he my ex-boyfriend now? That realization stung more than anything. But what else was I supposed to think? He'd filmed a video with London, and even if it was in the past, he should have told me. Warned me. Prepared me. Not let me stumble across it on the Internet like everyone else.

His profession already ensured I had to share him with the world. Anyone could Google him and see him in his underwear, or in any number of provocative poses, but this was way too much to handle. I wasn't cut out for this life. I didn't want a boyfriend who was a celebrity, a media target, or one with so many salacious secrets. It wasn't healthy.

The niggling feeling in my gut was back in full force. This relationship wasn't going to work. As much as I'd try to force it, to prove to myself that Ben fit into my life, this was the universe's way of showing me it wouldn't ever work. I needed to cut my losses now. But first, I wanted to lose myself in grief. Slamming my eyes closed to force away the images of him with another woman, I curled into a ball and quietly sobbed. I sobbed for what I'd seen, and I sobbed for my poor smashed-up heart. It'd never recover. I knew I'd always live with Ben in there and the realization terrified me.

17

Ben

"What do you think of this one?" I asked Bray, holding up an elaborately cut five-carat-diamond ring.

He shifted his weight, looking completely out of place at Tiffany in his worn jeans and scuffed-up Chucks. But I needed him here. I needed his opinion. "Ah . . . honestly? That's too much. Emmy's a simple girl, right?"

"Yeah." He was right. This was too much. I wanted the best for her. But she'd want something a little more understated. I wanted something significant on her finger. Something that said, *She's fucking taken*, but I needed to respect who she was. I continued scanning the rows of rings.

"What about this?" I held up a much simpler two-carat solitaire for him to inspect.

"Yeah. Actually, that's perfect."

Exactly what I was thinking. This would suit Emmy to a

T. It was simple, classic, timeless. It'd look beautiful on her finger. "I'll take it," I told the salesclerk.

I dropped the ring into his waiting palm, feeling proud, excited, and optimistic. The thought of kneeling on one knee and sliding this ring onto Emmy's finger while gazing into her pretty blue eyes made me feel like a damn emotional fool. This is what people wrote love songs about. Entire novels. Shit. I needed to pull it together. I was getting fucking misty-eyed inside Tiffany's. What a fucking tool.

I couldn't wait to take Emmy out this weekend to celebrate, and I hoped when I pulled out the ring, she'd be surprised—in a good way. I'd only hinted at my openness to marriage, wanting to keep things a surprise.

"Wait. . . ." The salesclerk grinned up at me. "You're the guy from the video. Fuck me . . . London Burke . . . you're a lucky man. This ring for her?" He smiled at me, waiting for my answer.

It wasn't uncommon to be recognized, but I had no clue what he was talking about. And London? I hadn't dated London in years. "What video?"

He laughed and winked at me. "The video everyone's talking about. I saw it online this morning. That shit was hot."

Oh shit.

Braydon and I exchanged a look of horror.

Realization flooded me and I suddenly felt sick. The blurry sex tape we'd recorded while drunk two years ago. No way. It couldn't be. I'd destroyed my copy and London had sworn she deleted hers, too.

I swallowed the bitter taste in my mouth. Awareness burned in the back of my brain . . . something told me Fiona was behind the leak of the tape. I racked my brain, fighting to remember back to two years ago. I'd confided in her once I sobered up and realized that I'd fucking recorded a sex tape. I knew that if it got out, I'd need her help. At the time, in the stark light of morning, I'd regretted what London and I had done. Fiona had assured me that it'd never be discovered. We'd been in Singapore when we deleted the copy on my laptop. Only now I wondered if she could have saved a copy for herself somewhere. I would have never suspected her at the time. But now knowing how she truly felt about me, and knowing that we always had adjoining rooms back then, she had the opportunity and means and potentially the motivation, too. The thought sickened me.

I dashed from the store, pulling my phone from my pocket. I dialed Emmy's number.

No answer.

I tried her again.

Nothing.

And again.

Fuck.

I paced the sidewalk, traffic zooming past as I silently prayed she'd pick up, give me the chance to explain. I needed to do some major damage control before she found out about the video.

On the eighth ring, Ellie answered. "Yes?"

I stopped suddenly. "Is she there?"

"She is."

"Can I speak to her?" My heart was thumping like a god-damn racehorse.

"Ben, she knows. She saw the video."

Fuck. "I'm so sorry. Let me explain. Let me apologize."

"She can't talk right now."

"Please. Just put her on the phone."

"You've gone too far this time. Pushed her too much. She's cracked."

"Cracked?"

"Yeah. She's in bed crying herself to sleep. It's done. Just leave her be."

"I can't," I admitted. "She's my everything. She owns me. That video is from years ago, and London and I made it as a stupid joke. We swore we'd deleted it. I think Fiona released it as a last act of revenge. Please . . . we can't let her win." My voice cracked.

"You've fucked up too many times. She can't forgive this." Ellie hung up and I pressed a hand against the brick wall to steady myself. In the course of three minutes flat, my world had just crumbled.

Fuck that. I hailed the nearest cab, leaving Braydon shouting something from the jewelry shop behind me.

"Drive like the fucking wind and I'll tip you handsomely," I told the driver, then gave him Emmy's address in Queens.

When I reached her building I took the stairs two at a time, jogging up to her unit while my heart pounded erratically. Dread filled me. I just needed her to see me, to look into my eyes and let me explain.

Forcing a deep breath of air into my lungs, I knocked at the door and waited, stuffing my hands into my pockets.

Nothing happened for several long seconds, and I knew either Emmy or Ellie was peering through the peephole, deciding on whether or not to open the door.

Moments ticked past and I thought I heard whispering coming from inside.

I knocked again, more urgently this time. "Emmy, please. I know you're in there. Let me explain." My voice sounded steady but my stomach curled into a tight knot.

Silence.

I pounded against the door, desperation overtaking me. "Baby."

I beat my fists against the door for what seemed like forever until my knuckles were red and raw.

"Go away, Ben. It's over," Ellie called tersely through the door.

Tears filled my vision. It couldn't end like this. I slunk to the floor and sat there for hours, praying that the door would open, if not to see me, then at least because one of them needed to go out for something. I was certain once Emmy saw me, met my eyes, I could make her understand.

But that chance never came.

In the days that followed, my phone rang and rang, but it was never Emmy.

At Fiona's sixth call for the day, I finally picked up. "Yeah?"

"Love . . ." Her endearment for me hung in the air, feeling empty. "I saw the news and I've been trying to reach you. Are you okay?"

"I'm fucking fabulous," I bit out. Was she seriously asking me that? My sex tape had been leaked, likely by her, and my girlfriend had left me. London and I had spoken once when the news story broke and she'd apologized profusely. She'd said she had no clue how the video got out. I believed her. She wouldn't have intentionally leaked it—she was just as mortified as I was. Her publicist had released the obligatory statement requesting the public to respect her privacy during this difficult time.

"You need me to fix this for you. Emmy can't handle this level of PR, love. Let me handle this."

Her motivation for releasing the video became clear. It was her last-ditch effort to bring me back to her. If she thought I'd need her to fix this, she was wrong. She also assumed Emmy was still working for me. Emmy wasn't even speaking to me, but I was still paying her. I refused to stop that. Emmy would never suffer because of my fuck-ups. I called her non-stop, left voicemails until her mailbox was full, and yet still nothing. Utter silence on her end.

"Fiona . . ." I warned. I didn't need her help.

"Let me take care of it. I'll make it go away."

I didn't care about it going away. I just wanted Emmy back. The sex tape didn't bother me. The world knowing that I liked to fuck didn't matter. Losing my girl, my reason for breathing, did. Big fucking time. "I don't need your help. And in fact, give me one reason why I should believe you didn't leak this tape yourself."

"Darling . . ." She stumbled only slightly. "I would never hurt you. You have to believe that."

"I don't know what to believe anymore. All I know is London didn't release it, and I sure as fuck didn't."

A tense silence hung between us while I tried to get my breathing under control.

"Can I ask you something?" her voice was tiny, unsure, very unlike Fiona. "I run a multimillion-dollar business. We'd be a power couple. Unstoppable. What could you possibly want with her? What does she have to offer you?"

"Fiona, I'm not discussing this with you. I'm with Emmy. She's all I want. Let's not dredge this up again." I was pretty certain it wouldn't do Fiona any good to hear me pledge my love for Emmy.

"Don't you want a woman capable of being your equal?"

"She isn't my equal. She's better than I ever hope to be."

Her family, her positive outlook on life, her simple beauty. I wanted whatever she was willing to give me. I'd take it. Gladly. In an industry filled with vanity and looks-are-everything, Emmy never let the fame go to my head. She'd always treated me like a regular guy. Like a man who was meant to be cherished for the actual person I was inside and not some idol to be worshipped and gazed at from afar. It was the only real thing in my life. This sex-tape scandal only proved what I already knew. I wasn't near good enough for her.

"Ben?" she asked, filling the silence.

I said nothing. I'd said everything I had to say.

"I've got to go, Fiona. Good-bye." The tone to my voice was final and I knew she knew it, too.

The more I thought about it, the more I became convinced Fiona was behind the video's release. Though I knew I'd never be able to prove it. A woman scorned would go to great lengths to exact her revenge. I'd left her agency, taking the income she made from my bookings, and of course I'd called off our affair. Though to be fair, I'd done that before I even met Emmy. I think in Fiona's mind, though, the two events were related. She blamed Emmy for stealing me away. The truth was, I'd just had enough of her possessiveness over me. And I'd started to feel shady, sleeping with my boss and all.

I was done with her. The drama, the lies . . . all of it. She'd been good to me and my mother for a long time, but those days were done. It was time to move on. I just wished I knew how the fuck to do that.

18

Emmy

One Month Later

I knew I was getting on Ellie's last nerve but I couldn't help myself. I'd spent the entire month in sweatpants, moping around, moving from my bed to the couch and back again. I rarely ate a proper meal, preferring instead bowls of ice cream, sugary candy, soda, and chips. It was low-maintenance and easy to grab when I was sitting on my butt feeling sorry for myself. I refused to shower unless absolutely necessary and seldom went outside. It was nearly Christmas, and a beautiful white layer of fluffy snow blanketed the city, but all I wanted to do was hole up in my own private misery.

Ellie tried time and again to get me out for some fresh air and set my laptop on my lap to encourage me to look for a job, but I kept putting it off. I wasn't ready to face that this was my life. I wasn't ready to accept that I was no longer with Ben. Frustratingly enough, he continued to call my cell phone nonstop and had my regular pay direct-deposited into my bank account. And of course he still occupied my brain the majority of the time.

Each night before bed I fought the urge to break down and listen to the dozens of voice messages he'd left. But I couldn't. That might lead to me dialing his number and calling him back. I was desperate to hear his deep, gravelly, sleep-laced voice. It haunted my dreams. Instead, I did the only thing I could do. I called my mom. I'd put off telling anyone about the breakup. It was as if even speaking it aloud would make it real. More final.

The second I heard her voice I broke down in tears like a blubbering baby.

"Momma?"

"Emerson Jean, what is it?"

"Ben and I . . . we . . . broke up . . ." I sobbed.

"Oh, honey." She did her best to soothe and comfort me without asking too many prying questions, and for that I was grateful.

"We've been through too much, Mom. I just don't know if we're meant to be."

"Well that's for you to decide, honey. I know you seemed awfully happy when you were here."

"We were . . ."

"Let me tell you a little story," she said. "Grandma and

Grandpa Clarke were together sixty-seven years before he passed. They had a long and very happy marriage. But did you know they almost split up in the early years of their marriage?"

I shook my head. "I didn't know that." My grandparents were two of the most in-love people I'd ever known. They loved each other deeply, still held hands, laughed and kissed regularly right up until the end.

"Romance novels and movies paint a too-rosy picture. Real life has its ups and downs, honey. Ben has a past. So what? He's a public figure and all those mistakes are going to be made public. That's just how it goes. You have to decide what you want. What you can live with. Can you live with his past? Or can you live without him?"

I knew I couldn't live without him. But I also wasn't sure I was ready to forgive him just yet.

By morning, my swollen red eyes and ratty hair were a dead giveaway of the night I'd had. I dragged a quilt out to the couch and plopped down. I could hear Ellie in the kitchen and closed my eyes, silently praying she'd take pity on my poor soul and bring me a cup of coffee.

"All right. Enough." Ellie ripped my ratty old quilt from my legs. "You're getting off your ass today."

I fought for my blanket back, but seeing it was no use I just curled my legs up under me on the couch, frowning at her. "It's not that easy, Ells."

She sat down in the armchair across from me. "I get that

this is hard. Trust me. Men suck most of the time. But don't let him own you. Don't let him win."

I chewed on my lip, digesting her meaning. It made sense. I nodded.

"Good. Because I kind of set you up on a lunch date for tomorrow."

"What? Hell no. I'm not ready for that yet. Are you insane?"

She rolled her eyes. "Stop it. It's one date. With Todd from my work. He's harmless. You can do this. Getting back on the horse and all that shit."

I knew the saying well. It was one my grandmother used with me often while I was growing up. And I appreciated the sentiment. When your world fell apart, it was imperative to pick yourself up and dust yourself off. Of course that was easier said than done. I knew I needed to make an effort. Comb my hair, brush my damn teeth . . . but dating any other man besides Ben—that was the last thing on my mind. I wasn't interested. I didn't know if I'd ever be interested. "I'm not going, Ells. Call him and cancel."

"If you don't want Ben in your life, fine, I get it. But don't stop living it."

She was right. And though I was nowhere near ready to date, I nodded in agreement. Only to prove to myself that life could go on after Ben Shaw. "Fine. I'll go."

Ellie squealed. "That's my girl. He's nice. You'll have fun, trust me."

"He better not be an ass."

"It's just lunch. What could go wrong?"

What could go wrong? I thought of Ellie's harmless statement over and over again as I sat across from Todd. He'd shown up twenty minutes late to the chain restaurant he'd chosen we meet at. I'd been about to leave when he'd come inside in a huff, complaining loudly to the hostess about the slow service of the valet parking. I'd crossed my fingers and said a silent prayer that the short, stocky man with gel-slicked hair was not my date. Sadly, he was.

And now we were seated in a booth under the harsh lighting of a hanging lamp and I couldn't help noticing the sticky and dirty tablecloth, Todd's too-long nose hair, and his fingernails, which needed trimming. Not to mention how lonely and miserable I felt. Thankfully, though, we'd ordered drinks and I concentrated on sipping the giant margarita in front of me. Seriously, the size of the goblet of tequila and lime juice was my saving grace.

"You really like that thing, don't you?" he asked, taking a sip of his own drink.

Ben would have encouraged me to have whatever I wanted, not judge me for draining my cocktail in record time.

"Nerves, I guess," I answered, sliding the large goblet away from me.

He smiled warmly. "Haven't dated in a while?"

"Something like that."

I continued sipping my margarita while Todd prattled on about his job and I tried to appear interested.

"How hungry are you?" he asked. "Is an appetizer okay?" He closed his menu before I could answer.

I did the same. "That's fine." I didn't know that by appetizer he meant the free chips and salsa the server had delivered to the table. If this was dating, then no thanks. I'd been wined and dined around the world. Ben had set an impossibly high bar. It was almost as if he ensured no man would ever measure up to him. Realization struck like a sharp pain coursing through me. Todd was a regular guy, but after Ben no one would compare. It was my worst fear come to life. "I'll be right back," I murmured, sliding from the booth. I needed some air. Some space.

I stood outside the restaurant entrance and pulled in deep lungfuls of air. I just wanted to go home, change into my pajamas, and erase this date from my memory. Unfortunately, moments later, Todd strolled out looking for me.

"Hey," I said.

He placed his hand against my lower back. "Are you okay?"

It happened so fast I thought my mind was playing tricks on me. I blinked rapidly, trying to process what I was seeing. Ben had Todd by the shirt collar and was hauling him away from me. My heart twisted at the sight of him. Ben dragged Todd backward, shoving his back against the wall. Todd let out an *oomph*.

"Get your fucking hands off her," Ben growled.

"Ben!" I tugged at his arms, trying to get him to release my date, but he didn't budge an inch. His entire body was tensed and ready to fight. "Let him go," I begged again. He was causing a scene.

Sad hazel eyes found mine and everything else ceased. The sights and sounds of the street fell away, and it was just us. A man and woman so beautifully wrong for each other it hurt. My lungs screamed for oxygen and I gulped a breath of air. "Let him go," I repeated, my senses returning.

"He was touching you," he said softly. His gentle tone with me was at complete odds with the roughness of his grasp on Todd. "You looked upset."

"He's my date."

"You're on a fucking date?" His hands dropped from Todd's collar and he stumbled several steps back like he'd been burned. Forcing fingers into his messy hair, Ben's agony was almost pitiable. An apology was on the tip of my tongue until I remembered his actions had pushed me down this path.

"Todd Hammerstein." My awkward date who I wanted to disappear thrust his hand out toward Ben.

"With this guy?" Ben asked. He made no move to return the handshake, his fingers flexing at his sides. He obviously wanted to hit something. Preferably my date. I felt like I was watching him for the first time. Seeing straight inside his soul. How badly he needed love. And how much it hurt him to see me with someone else.

"How have you been?" he asked, turning to face me.

"Shitty. You?"

"The same," he admitted.

"What are you doing here?"

"I brought my mother shopping." He glanced to a lingerie boutique across the street. "She's in there."

Oh.

His mom was here from Australia. "Did she come for Christmas?"

He rubbed the back of his neck. "Sort of. I haven't been, ah, doing so well with the sex-tape scandal, and then you leaving me, so she came to town for a visit."

Todd's eyebrows shot up and he cleared his throat loudly. Both Ben and I continued to ignore him.

"I can't live that way. Seeing you splashed all over the tabloids like that nearly destroyed me."

"I know. And I wish I could take that back. But I did that before I met you. It was years ago. I can't help what's in the past, only what's in the present. Only what I do now. That's all we can control. And you're here with another man."

I swallowed roughly, unsure of what to say.

It didn't occur to me right away that the woman who appeared at Ben's side was his mother. She looked far too young to have a twenty-three-year-old son, but as soon as my eyes fell on her I recognized Dakota Shaw. She was tall and fit and very pretty, with waves of sandy blond hair cascading over her shoulders.

My brain cataloged the few similarities between them. They each had thick, dark eyelashes, wide-set eyes, and full mouths. A gorgeous family, to be sure.

"Well, this must be the girl who stole my baby's heart."

"Mom," Ben warned, his voice low.

She sighed and opened her arms. "Okay, I'll play nice. I'm Dakota, Ben's mom. Come here, then."

I returned her hug, my head spinning with what she must think. Did she know about her darling son's sex tape?

Ben took the collection of shopping bags from her arms, ever the good, doting son. This was a totally new side of him and it was fascinating to watch.

"Can I take you for a drink?" Ben asked, gazing at me steadily. "I'm not ready to let you disappear yet."

"I don't think that's a good idea."

"Oh, honey, it's one drink. Your friend can even come." Dakota motioned to Todd.

"Actually, this is too weird for me," Todd spoke up. "I'm sorry, but I'm going to bail. Can you get a ride home?"

Gee thanks. I scowled at my date. The jackass was going to turn tail and run.

"Henry will take you anywhere you'd like to go," Ben said.

I nodded to Todd, too numb to argue right now.

Soon we were seated at an elegant bar on the Upper East Side. I sat between Ben and his mom. Dakota ordered a mineral water with a slice of lemon. I was guessing she was still maintaining her sobriety. Immediately falling back into old habits, I allowed Ben to order me a glass of wine. A deliciously light glass of Pinot Grigio.

"Have you eaten?" he asked, keeping his eyes on mine. I shook my head. I'd expected to have lunch with Todd, but that hadn't happened. "A couple of menus, please," Ben said to the bartender.

We ordered lunch and nibbled on grilled tuna and spring salad while making small talk. Ben's mom was actually lovely and sweet. I didn't know what I'd been expecting, but maybe age had calmed her. It was obvious that she loved her son deeply. Even if she hadn't been the most maternal parent while he was growing up. She fussed over him, offering him food from her plate and chastising him for not eating enough. It was sweet.

"That ring would've looked beautiful on her." Dakota shook her head, looking at my naked ring finger. "It's a shame."

Ring? My heart tripped in my chest. Ben hadn't gotten me a ring . . . couldn't have? Could he?

His jaw tensed and he briefly shook his head in an attempt to silence his mother. Rather than make eye contact with me, his gaze was cast downward into his glass of scotch. Frown lines creased his forehead as he swirled the amber-colored liquor, looking deep in thought.

I wanted to say something, to ask what she meant, but of course I couldn't. The words dried up in my throat and I had to swallow a gulp of my wine to get my windpipe working again. I tried to take stock of how I even felt about this. It was what I'd wanted all along—a commitment from Ben. Just him and I. Knowing that he had considered proposing—making it official—made my heart palpitate unevenly. After everything we'd been through—Fiona's desperate attempts at winning him over and his sex-tape scandal, I didn't know if too much trust had been broken. But my heart didn't think so. Whether or not I wanted to, I still loved him deeply. I knew a part of me always would. But forgiving him, moving past this . . . that would take time. And, honestly, I couldn't see myself being that forgiving anytime soon.

Ben's posture told me the conversation was done but when he waved to the bartender, signaling for the check, I knew things were final. I got up and excused myself for the bathroom. I needed a moment to gather my thoughts before facing him. My pink cheeks and splotchy chest were a dead giveaway of the emotions raging inside me. Half of me wanted to slap him; the other half wanted to throw myself into his arms and never let him go. It was still a question of which half would win.

19

Ben

Emmy's pink-flushed skin and accelerated pulse thrumming in her neck told me something about the ring excited her. And that fact roared through me. Did Emmy want my ring on her finger? Would she say yes if I asked? Would she throw herself into my arms? Believing there might be a chance to win her back made my heart kick up a notch. There was only one way to find out. And she was sitting here having a drink with me after all. Though she'd been on a date with some douche bag named Todd, she'd stayed with me. I was the one feeding her, making sure she'd get home safe and sound. Not that asshole. He didn't care about her, didn't love her like I did. She was my everything, my reason for breathing, for getting up in the morning, hoping she'd call. If she hadn't wanted to see me, she would have left. Emmy wasn't too shy to refuse me. I knew that by now. I wouldn't go down without a fight.

I could only hope that she'd change her mind, understand

that the mistakes of my past were done. If she'd just let me talk to her, explain, it might help. But I wasn't about to discuss my sexual past with my mother sitting right next to us. I needed just one more chance with her and I had to make it a good one.

The thought consumed me and I knew I needed time to process. Struggling to keep my game face in place, I requested the check. I needed time to fucking think. Sort this mess out. Probably talk to Bray. And I sure as shit needed to talk to my mom. She should not have said what she did.

The three of us wandered from the restaurant and were waiting on the sidewalk for Henry to arrive when my mom excused herself to use the restroom one last time.

I turned to face Emmy, resisting the urge to pull her body into mine to shield her from the cold. "Will you give me a chance to explain?"

She shrugged. "I've given you lots of chances."

"I know. And I need just one more opportunity."

Emmy bit her lip, thinking it over. "I had to find out at the same time as the rest of the world about my boyfriend starring in an adult film. I hated that."

"I fucked up. I know. I should have told you sooner, but honestly I'd forgotten all about that video. Hell, I didn't even think it still existed."

Her gaze wandered from mine and she blinked back tears. I wanted to go to her, to hold her, to comfort her, but I'd lost that right, so I stood there like a useless sack of crap, wishing things could be different.

"In the third grade I had a French tutor named Collette. I used to pretend I needed extra help on my spelling tests so she'd lean over my desk and I could look down her shirt."

Her eyes snapped to mine. "What?"

"Yeah. And when I was fourteen, my mom brought me to Lincoln Center for the BCBG Max Azria show. I snuck backstage and peeked around a barrier and watched the models undressing in between their exits."

"Why are you telling me this?"

"Because. I never want to hide anything from you ever again. I've done things I'm not proud of—things I'd prefer stay in the past. I won't let anything interfere with our future, so I'll tell you anything and everything you want to know."

"Ben, you don't have to do that. I just . . ."

"What Emmy? Tell me how to fix this."

"I can't. I don't know. You broke my trust."

I took her hand. "Let me build it back."

"Ready, darling?" My mom appeared beside us after returning from the restroom.

Emmy's hand went limp in mine. "Yes, I'm ready to go home."

I hated leaving things this way—so unfinished. My jaw tightened as I opened the door and helped my mom and Emmy inside the waiting car.

Emmy was silent and contemplative on the ride to Queens and I feared it was because there was nothing more to say.

When she exited the car, watching her turn her back and

walk away was the hardest thing I'd ever done. Shielding herself against the snow, Emmy jogged up the front steps to her building and out of my life.

"You want me to do what?" Porter asked.

"I need your help with Emmy. I wouldn't have come to you if I didn't need you. But I do, man."

Porter scrubbed his hands over his face. "I came to New York. I'm here. And I appreciate the airline ticket and hotel room, but I don't know about the rest. Emmy makes up her own mind. I'll talk to her, but she'll have to decide what she wants."

At Braydon's suggestion of asking Emmy's father for her hand in marriage, I'd gone a step further. I'd flown her whole family to New York City—the first time for all three of them—and put them up in a suite at the Waldorf Astoria. It was a little over the top for my tastes—too ornate—but I knew they'd appreciate staying at a historic New York landmark. Porter and I were currently having a beer at a bar around the corner from the hotel. He and I had some lost ground to make up since he'd caught me and Emmy in the act on her parents' couch over Thanksgiving.

I knew in addition to speaking with her father—man to man—that I needed to win over her brother, too. He and I weren't exactly on speaking terms, and I couldn't say I blamed him. I couldn't imagine any scenario where he didn't want to punch me in the jaw.

"I want you to know I love your sister. I'm not giving her up. I'm never letting her go, and I give you my word that she'll always be loved and taken care of." I met his eyes, sincerity in my voice. I didn't care that I probably sounded like the world's biggest pussy. I loved her with my whole being, and I'd do anything to get her back.

Porter swallowed a gulp of his beer and released a deep sigh.

Her dad was a piece of cake compared to Porter. When I'd taken him and Sue to lunch yesterday, he'd been unsure at first, saying it was up to Emmy, but he wouldn't stand in the way of her happiness. After lunch, he'd shaken my hand, clapped me on the back, and said as long as I promised to love her and care for her the way she deserved, then the past was in the past and he'd happily give me his blessing to ask her. Porter, on the other hand, was less than forgiving. Whereas Emmy's parents had hints only of my past indiscretions, Porter had come right out and asked me about the tape. I thought I'd dodged the bullet well, telling him it was a one-time mistake and I'd been told the video had been destroyed.

Porter's eyes followed the backside of a passing waitress. "Are we done here?"

"Actually I was hoping you could help me arrange something else."

His eyes flickered back to mine with interest.

20

Emmy

Pulling on a pair of cream-colored wool tights and a soft gray knit dress, I checked myself in the mirror one last time. I looked tired. My curled hair and mascaraed lashes couldn't hide the fact that I was miserable without Ben. My skin was pale and my expression was sullen. Oh well. It would have to do.

Ellie had succeeded in talking me into meeting her for a Christmas Eve drink in Manhattan. She promised me it would be relaxed and low key and said that the little twinkling white lights and Christmas decorations would lift my spirits. Either that or the rum-spiked eggnog would.

I was making an effort, just like I'd promised her I would. And I was trying, I really was. I'd been showering regularly and had been eating better, too. On the outside I appeared to be healing. But since seeing Ben randomly on the Upper

East Side last week, my foolish heart latched onto how sweet and attentive he'd been, how sad and miserable he'd looked without me, the dark circles under his eyes indicating a lack of sleep. It tugged on my heart. But I was being strong. Even if it meant I had to give myself daily pep talks and cry myself to sleep each night.

To make matters worse, for the first time ever, I wasn't going home for Christmas. My mom and dad had made plans with friends from church. She said that's what empty nesters did, and since I was home for Thanksgiving, she didn't think I'd be coming home for Christmas, too. It was probably just as well since I was willing to bet the memories of Ben's last visit to my parents' home would still be too fresh. The way he'd accepted my family and our lifestyle meant so much to me. But I couldn't let myself focus on that now.

I slid on my brown knee-high boots and grabbed my purse. After bundling up and heading outside, I opted to spring for a cab rather than take the subway. For some unknown reason Ben had continued paying me my full salary, and being a hermit for the past several weeks I'd hardly spent a dime. I crossed my mitten-covered fingers that I could successfully hail a cab. Seconds later a yellow taxi pulled to a stop on the curb next to me. The simple accomplishment did wonders for my self-esteem. I pushed my shoulders back and slid inside the warm car. "The Waldorf Astoria, please," I told the driver. The bar I was meeting Ellie at was inside the historic hotel.

When I arrived, a uniformed doorman greeted me and pulled open the doors of the bustling hotel. I wandered inside the massive and elaborately decorated lobby. The scent of leather and citrus furniture polish was in the air as I made my way toward the entrance of the bar.

I found Ellie sitting alone, chatting casually with the bartender. When she spotted me she hopped up from her stool. "Oh, good, you're here!" She slung her purse over her shoulder.

"Are we getting a drink?" I noticed the distinct lack of beverages in front of her.

"I've arranged for us to have a tour of the hotel. This place is supposed to be really cool."

I groaned. "I don't want a tour. I just want to sit like a lump." Getting myself dressed and out the door was a big enough adventure. Now I just wanted the drink I'd been promised.

"It'll be fun. Stop whining," she commanded, picking up her coat from the stool beside her and draping it over her arm.

"Let's just get a drink and go home. Put on pajamas and order Chinese food," I begged.

"No, come on. It'll just be a quick tour."

Knowing that arguing with a determined-looking Ellie was pointless, I dutifully followed her to the elevators.

She pressed the button for the top floor and grinned widely. She was being quiet, too quiet. And something about her odd behavior was setting off warning bells inside my head. I couldn't take another setup, and I would have no problem telling her no and leaving if that's what this was. I wasn't ready to date—now, or maybe ever. My life post-Ben was still in a tailspin. She just needed to accept that.

When the elevator doors opened I expected to find a hotel employee there, and maybe a group of tourists for the supposed tour, but the hallway was quiet and empty. I followed Ellie across the hall to a set of French doors. She knocked once and the door was pulled open. My brother Porter stood there, smiling back at me.

"Porter!" I squealed and threw myself into his arms.

"Hey, sis," he greeted me, his southern drawl more pronounced than mine.

"What are you doing here?" I slugged his shoulder. How dare he come to New York and not tell me. He opened the door wider and I spotted my parents standing in the beautiful living room behind him. "Mom? Dad?" I crossed the threshold, now thoroughly baffled, and gave them both hugs. I blinked back a rush of tears as emotions roared through me.

"Hi honey," my mom said, planting a kiss on my forehead.

"What's going on?" My eyes danced around the lavishly decorated hotel suite. A large, bushy evergreen adorned with twinkling lights and red-and-gold ribbons stood in the corner and filled the room with the lovely scent of crisp pine needles. A glass cart held a combination of crystal decanters and stemware. The coffee table was lined with various appetizers and finger foods.

"We're here to celebrate Christmas in New York with you, honey," my mom said, smoothing my curls back from my face. My dad, Ellie, and Porter stood in the center of the living room, watching my confused expression.

"I don't understand . . ." My eyes scanned the room, following my mom's softening gaze.

Ben.

He stood tall and devastatingly handsome, dressed in a shirt and tie in the dining alcove just off the living space.

"Hi," he said simply.

Had he arranged this whole thing? Flown my parents and brother here? Rented this lavish room? Filled it with a live Christmas tree and delectable foods? Coerced Ellie into dragging me up here? My heart stuttered in my chest. It was too much. He was too much. Knowing that he was here, fighting for me, trying to prove his love for me, filled me with longing. Silent tears rolled down my cheeks as I drank him in.

Ben crossed the room in three long strides, drawing me into his arms. His embrace lifted my feet clear off the floor and held me against him. He crushed me against his chest like he was never going to let me go. I hung there suspended in the air, big ugly tears streaming down my cheeks. I couldn't control the emotions warring inside me, so I didn't even try. I had no idea what his gesture meant or where we'd go from here. All I knew is that I'd never felt more loved and cherished, and he hadn't even said more than a single word yet. He'd spoken to me through his actions—what I'd wanted from him all along. He'd brought me my family, he'd brought me Christmas, knowing how important family traditions were to me. It choked me up and made my heart ache.

After several long moments of just holding me silently and letting me cry, Ben set me on my feet.

"Can we talk?" he asked softly.

I was all too aware of the roomful of people surrounding us, collectively holding their breath, waiting to see what I'd do. I caught my lower lip between my teeth and thought about what to say. How could I tell the man I was desperately in love with no? That I couldn't have my heart broken again? I swallowed the dryness in my throat. How could I explain how completely he'd broken me? That I'd considered getting on antidepressants just to get over him? It probably wasn't a good sign that my heart, mind, and body still wanted him, as much as I might try to deny it.

I turned to face our spectators. "This may get kind of loud, so if you're squeamish, leave now." When my gaze returned to Ben he was smiling crookedly.

"This way." He took my hand and led me down the suite's hall. We passed several doors on our way to the end of the hall. Lord, how many bedrooms did this suite have? Closing us inside a lavish bedroom with a queen-sized bed, writing desk, and chaise lounge, Ben caged me in against the wall, one hand splayed across my hip, one tilting my mouth up to meet his. His kiss was possessive, evocative, and hard. He was kissing me as though it was our last. The thought filled me with remorse. My brain screamed at me. I couldn't lose him, but I needed to tell him what was on my mind before I lost myself completely in his kiss.

I pushed hard against his chest to break the connection and drew a shaky gulp of air.

Ben's knuckles stroked my jaw. "You okay, baby?"

I pushed his hand away. "Don't baby me."

"What? You warned them this could get loud . . . I thought you wanted . . ." His brow knitted in confusion.

Oh my God. He thought I wanted sex? Ha! "Yes, loud because I'd be yelling at you."

"Oh."

Yeah. Oh. "Ben . . ." I ran my fingers through my hair, trying to calm myself. "Bringing my family here . . . planning this surprise is incredible, but it doesn't fix things between us."

His face fell.

"Don't you dare let me find out things that big about your life on the Internet."

He nodded sheepishly. "I'm so sorry. I'll spend the rest of forever making it up to you, if you just let me."

"I don't need to know that you had a crush on your teacher in the third grade. What I need is to trust you."

"I know, baby. I know. I promise you that you can." I'd never seen his expression so somber, his eyes so sad. "These last few weeks have been the worst of my life, Emmy. I can't lose you. You're mine. And I'm yours."

My heart clenched in my chest and I drew a deep breath. His sincerity, his masculine scent, the pain reflected in his eyes was too much. I turned away from him, gazing out the window to the city blanketed by snow. Things looked so simple on the outside; traffic continued zooming past, lights burned brightly in the distance, people huddled into their coats for warmth on the sidewalk below. Life went on. There was beauty, heartache, and love so bottomless you felt it deep in your core. That was the love Ben and I had found. We'd hit some bumpy patches, sure, but my mom's advice resonated in my head. Perhaps it was all part of life. There were ups and downs, love and loss. And I knew in my heart I wasn't ready to give him up. Not over a stupid video he'd made years ago before he even knew me. I'd just need to grow thicker skin if I wanted to be with him.

I turned to face him in the silent room. "There aren't going to be any more women, any more stories coming out of the woodwork, are there?"

"No ma'am." His voice was firm.

I paced the room, planting my hands on my hips. "Thank God you only slept with three girls before me—you seem to make stupid decisions where sex is involved. And don't think I won't track down the third girl and grill her if necessary. Because I will." I jabbed a finger in his direction.

"No, that's not needed."

I shot him a warning glare that said I wasn't above doing just that. I knew Bray would help me if I needed it.

"Listen, Emmy, I'm trying to tell you, this last month has been the hardest of my life. I can't survive without you. You're my world, baby. Please say you can forgive me."

His hand found mine and he laced our fingers together, joining us from wrist to elbow. The warmth of his skin, the weight of his hand in mine, the burn in his gaze all served to remind me I really was his. And I couldn't live without him, either. Looking into his hazel gaze felt like coming home. No way was I willing to give that up.

I lifted on my toes and pressed a kiss to his surprised mouth. "I forgive you," I murmured.

His mouth slanted against mine and his tongue sought entrance, lightly stroking my own. God, I'd missed him. I missed everything about him. His sweet kisses, his filthy murmurings in my ear, the feel of his firm body pressed to mine. I was stupid to think a video recorded years ago was enough to come between us. He held my jaw in his hands and kissed me like his life depended on it. I realized something in that moment. I wouldn't let anything come between us ever again. We'd weather whatever storms life delivered *together*.

His hands wandered from my face to my neck, sliding down over my shoulders, my lower back, and down to my bottom, which he cupped in his palms to haul me closer. "Don't ever leave me again, baby. Ever. Promise me."

"I promise," I whispered in between kisses.

Being back in Ben's arms gave me solace. Not the kind of fairytale love that the movies portrayed. What we had was real. We were real. We made mistakes, held grudges, and then moved on. It actually gave me peace of mind to know that.

"Come on, your family's probably wondering where we are," he said, releasing his tight hold on me ever so slightly.

Remembering that my mom, dad, and brother were here in New York warmed my heart. "Thank you for bringing them to me. That was incredibly thoughtful and sweet of you."

Taking my hand in his once again, he led me back to the living room. My mom and Ellie rushed to my side, questioning smiles ghosting their lips.

"Everything okay?" my mom asked.

Keeping one hand possessively curled around my hip, Ben looked to me to answer.

"Everything's great, Mom." I gave Ellie a reassuring look, too, letting her know there were no hard feelings for dragging me over here.

My dad and brother remained planted across the room, watching us as they quietly sipped their drinks. Watching me with Ben, my dad's mouth curled into a lazy smile, and while Porter still looked guarded, he nodded something in silent agreement to Ben.

Now that I was more relaxed I took in the room more thoroughly. The ten-foot evergreen tree smelled intoxicating and made the room cozy and inviting. I didn't know how he'd managed to get a Christmas tree delivered to a hotel room, but I knew there was nothing he wouldn't do for me. The thought filled my heart with love.

My mom, ever the hostess, ensured everyone had a cocktail in their hands and encouraged us to eat. The hors d'oeuvres did look delicious and smelled even better.

"Are you hungry?" Ben asked.

"A little," I admitted.

He released his hold on me just long enough to prepare me a small plate of bruschetta, spicy shrimp on skewers, and mushrooms stuffed with feta cheese.

Yum.

I accepted the plate and nibbled on a bite of shrimp. The

emotional journey over the past hour had left me surprisingly hungry.

Ben helped himself to a shrimp from the platter then returned to my side, his large hand once again finding my hip to curl around me, possessive and sure.

After we'd eaten all the appetizers and devoured the mini chocolate cheesecakes for dessert, my mom shuffled us to sit down around the tree.

My parents, Ellie, and Porter sunk into the inviting sofa and armchairs while I sat cross-legged on the floor next to the tree. It was the spot I always took at home on Christmas morning to pass out the presents. Ben settled next to me on an ottoman.

"Too bad I didn't know you guys were coming. I don't have any gifts for you," I commented.

"That's okay, honey. Christmas isn't about the gifts. I'm just so glad we're together."

"Me too." My eyes found Ben's.

"Besides, Ben gave us the best gift of all: being here together." My mom smiled warmly at him. Oh yeah, my mom was sold. Hook, line, and sinker. He tended to have that effect on women.

He was still watching me intently, making me feel so incredibly cherished and special. "I think there is one present on the tree." He pointed to a branch near the center of the tree and I saw that he was right. Nestled among the pine needles was a tiny turquoise-colored box.

I felt the air around us shift. My mom leaned forward in her seat and Ellie held her breath. What was going on?

Ben rose to his feet and plucked the little box from the tree, then turned to face me, looking contemplative. Brilliant hazel eyes locked on mine and one hand lovingly stroked my cheek as he stood before me.

"Before you came along, I didn't know there was a piece of me missing. But there was. You've taken a place in my life, in my heart, that was empty before."

A stray tear escaped my eye and rolled along my cheek. Ben's thumb caught it and he smiled at me lightly before continuing. "You've enriched my life, made it more complete, and I don't want to spend any more of my days without you by my side. I love you with my whole heart."

My heart galloped in my chest, watching this beautiful man pour his heart out to me. My mom was now actively crying and my confused brain scrambled to try to make sense of this moment.

He dropped down onto both knees and kneeled before me, looking deep into my eyes. He slowly opened the box. "Will you be my wife, Emerson Jean?"

Big tears leaked from my eyes and my heart tripped over itself at hearing those words fall from Ben's mouth. It was everything I'd wanted and more.

But not like this. Not because he felt backed into a corner and needed to make some grand gesture to win me back. I wanted to shout yes, to throw myself into his embrace, to knock him to the floor and kiss him senseless. But the little annoying voice in the back of my head refused to pipe down.

Ben's confidence faltered, and I saw his jaw tense as he waited for me to answer.

Shit.

I knew how this man was with rejection, and I wasn't rejecting him . . . I just needed to talk to him about this. To be sure this was what he wanted.

"Emmy," he whispered, his voice a hoarse plea. "Do you want some privacy?"

I nodded.

He lifted me from the floor and carried me to the back bedroom we'd been in only moments before.

He set me on my feet, cupping my cheeks. "Baby?" Ben's voice broke and his eyes were filled with worry. "Please talk to me . . ."

I stood there uselessly sobbing because I'd just ruined my own proposal. Why hadn't I just said yes and then talked to him later in private? I'd taken what should have been a beautiful moment and turned it into drama. We had a roomful of people down the hall probably wondering what in the world was going on, and I had a wounded and hurt man standing in front of me.

"Fuck," he roared, shutting the door firmly behind us. "I should've never planned this elaborate thing in front of your family. I'm sorry, baby. Tell me why you're crying. Tell me how to fix it."

I drew a deep gulp of air and wiped the remnants of my ruined mascara from under my eyes, searching for a way to fix this.

Ben

Watching Emmy cry big, soggy tears broke my fucking heart. I wasn't sure how I'd managed to mess up this proposal, but somehow I had. A sob bubbled up her throat and broke from her lips. I held her, stroked her back, and let her cry. At least she wasn't pushing me away. I held her and swayed with her in my arms, letting her tears soak my shirt while lightly rubbing her back. It tore me up seeing her like this.

She finally took a sobering breath and stepped back. Her cheeks were wet with tears, her eyes red and swollen.

"Emmy, baby. Talk to me."

Crossing the room, she sat down on the bed. "I will. I just . . . need a minute." Her eyes briefly met mine, and what I saw there made my pulse sprint. Fear. Confusion. And uncertainty.

I nodded and waited, unable to do anything else. I could practically see the wheels turning in her head as she fought to organize her thoughts. I had no idea what had conflicted her so badly, but it was obvious she was struggling.

"Let me get you a glass of cool water." I stepped into the adjoining bath and filled a glass tumbler with cold tap water, if only for a moment to break the intensity humming between us.

Glancing into the bathroom mirror, the man staring back at me was just as much of a mess. My skin was pale and lifeless. I looked like shit. Fuck, I felt like shit without Emmy. I didn't think she ever understood how badly I needed her. I inhaled deeply, knowing that I'd need to search inside myself to find the right words to get through to her.

Moments later, I returned to her side with the glass of water and a box of tissues. She accepted each and after wiping her cheeks and blowing her nose, she took a sip of the water then handed the glass back to me.

"Thank you. Sit down," she instructed me, now slightly more composed. She patted the bed and I lowered myself down beside her.

"You know I'd never intentionally hurt you. You know that, right?"

She nodded slowly.

"I want us to work. I've cut Fiona out of my life. I thought severing that tie was all we needed to finally move forward as just us. I never thought that a video I recorded two years ago would come between us."

She sucked her lower lip into her mouth, so quiet and unsure.

"Tell me why you're crying," I coaxed, unsure if I should take her hand. I clenched my fists at my sides instead.

"Because."

Using two fingers, I lifted her chin, bringing her eyes up to meet mine. "Because why baby?"

"Because . . . this future with you . . . it's everything I've ever wanted."

"And . . ." I prompted.

She sniffed, her chin quivering. "And, I know this isn't you. It's not what you want, and I won't pressure you. I won't have you do this—make this grand gesture just to gain my forgiveness over your sex tape."

Holy shit. Her words felt like a punch to the gut. "That's what you thought this was? Some makeup gift? Some penance for my sins?"

She nodded carefully.

"I'm not good with pretty words, but I promise you I meant every word of that proposal. I want you with me always. I need you like I've never needed anything before. How can you not see that?"

"I believe you. I just can't go into this thinking you're doing it for the wrong reasons."

Realization struck me and hope ballooned in my chest. "Baby, I'm a selfish bastard, trust me. I'm going into this for all the wrong reasons. Because I want you to be mine. Forever. I can't let you go. I want us to vow that we'll be together because I can't lose you. I bought your ring before the tape even came out. I knew I wanted to marry you months ago. I've been trying desperately to get you to move in with me."

"Bennn . . ."

The sound of her whimpering my name was the sweetest

sound. It signaled her defenses falling away and her letting herself give in.

I could tell she was nervous but only because she thought I was proposing for the wrong reasons. I needed her to know how incredibly special she was to me. I gazed into her eyes, holding her face carefully a few inches from mine. "You're amazing. I love everything about you." I lightly stroked her jawline. "I love how soft you are. And I love the way you smell." I pressed my nose and mouth to her neck, tasting as I went. "I want to kiss every part of you," I whispered against her neck. She let out a soft moan at my words. "And I can. Because you're mine." She smiled up at me, relaxing a slight bit more. "So beautiful," I murmured against her lips.

I sunk to my knees in front of her, lifting her left hand to my lips. I kissed her naked ring finger and let my teeth lightly graze the soft flesh. I wanted her to understand that this finger was mine to mark.

Emmy's eyes widened as the meaning behind my gesture sunk in. Her breathing hitched and she bit her bottom lip.

"Lie back," I murmured, urging her back onto the bed and arranging the pillows behind her. She leaned against them so she was resting before me. I wanted her to be comfortable and at ease. She'd accepted my explanation, but that still didn't mean she'd said yes to my proposal. Fuck, I wished there was a playbook for this. I was out of my element. Big time.

"Close your eyes," I whispered.

She obeyed, letting her eyes slip closed.

She was so stunning laying there waiting for me. Long

eyelashes resting against her cheeks, delicate nose, the familiar slope of her chin, and the slight outline of collarbones at her neckline. Desire sliced through me. I wanted to do bad things to her and cherish her at the same time. My mind reeled with what to do first.

I brought my hands to her face, cradling her jaw and softly stroking her cheeks with my thumbs. "So soft." I leaned over her and nibbled on her bottom lip. I felt her mouth lift in a smile.

"Mmm. That feels nice," she breathed.

"I want to make you happy."

She let out a happy little moan. A good start.

I pressed a tender kiss to her mouth and licked at her lips until they parted, sucking her tongue into my mouth. She inhaled sharply at the surprise of my tongue sucking hers, and her eyes flew open before slowly drifting closed again. We kissed passionately for several minutes and my entire body relaxed into hers. "I want to take care of your every need," I whispered, breaking the kiss.

I'd wanted tonight to be perfect. This proposal meant everything to me, and now that the moment had passed I was desperate to get it back. To somehow recapture the magic. I lay down beside her, lacing our left hands. Her fingers tightened around mine. "I love you, Emmy. Let me make you my wife and love you for the rest of my life."

She looked up at me and smiled, murmuring the three best words I'd ever heard. "Where's my ring?"

21

Emmy

Six Months Later

"What are you still doing working?" Ellie stormed into my office, heels clicking loudly across the polished wood floors. "I've been blowing up your phone for the past hour. Get your booty outta that chair."

I glanced up from my computer screen, pausing just briefly in my work before letting my fingers resume tapping against the keys. I didn't want to lose my train of thought. "One sec. I just have a few more emails to send out."

"News flash, sweetie, you're getting married tomorrow," Ellie chuckled.

An unstoppable smile overtook my mouth and I grinned at her. I wondered if I should feel nervous or scared . . . but I only felt excitement. Ben and I had been living together for several months now and had never been happier. We'd opened the office to his charity last month and things had gone from busy to crazy. Thank God for my mom and Ellie's help with wedding planning. And Ben took on the responsibility of planning our honeymoon. I never would have survived otherwise. I felt a bit guilty about keeping on Magda to cook and clean, but the extra help had been a godsend.

I clicked send on the last email to my assistant. I vowed to never use brief, terse messages scribbled on Post-it notes to communicate with her, as was Fiona's method when I was her assistant. Instead I treated her like a human with a functioning brain. I just wanted to make sure she knew all of the vital things to get done in our absence for the next few weeks.

"Just about ready." I glanced up to see Ellie touring the small office Ben had rented me uptown. It was just a large loft with light, airy windows and pale wood floors. The walls were still stark white and the furniture basic, but it was perfect. He stopped in a few times a week and worked alongside me, the modeling jobs becoming less and less frequent, which suited us both fine. Now that we'd set up our charity, it was where we both wanted to devote our time.

I powered down my laptop and straightened the papers on my desk. No sense leaving the place trashed. I took pride in what I did. It was work that mattered.

After talking for months about which worthy cause we'd devote our time to, Ben decided on starting a charity for children who needed surgery and couldn't afford it. His organization funded plastic surgeries and medical procedures for children in need. We'd worked with families on things like cleft palates and reconstructive surgeries. My days were spent on the phone with hospitals and insurance companies, finding donors, and connecting with families. And lots of mundane things, too, like figuring out Web-hosting, answering mountains of emails, and making pot after pot of coffee to fuel us.

The glitz and the glamour of the modeling world had been replaced with helping children gain a positive self-image in the most basic of ways. By helping them get the care they needed and deserved. It filled my heart to know we were helping families, that we were making a difference in the lives of others.

I had the best job in the world. And the man I loved deeply right by my side. Except for tonight. Tonight was girl time with Ellie, and Ben was meeting up with Braydon for a drink.

"Last chance . . . instead of dinner reservations we could hit up a male strip club . . ." Ellie smiled wickedly.

"I have zero interest in going to a strip club, but thanks." Besides, I knew it wasn't my last chance. Ben wouldn't care if I suddenly woke up one day and told him I wanted to check that off my bucket list. He'd shared me with his friend, for goodness sake. Not that Ellie needed to know all that. She already hated Braydon for some strange reason. I didn't want to tell her about the threesome. I had no clue how she'd react.

"Fine. Boring it is. Dinner, drinks, and girl time."

"Sounds perfect to me." Ben and I had agreed to spend tonight apart in anticipation of making our wedding day that much more special when we were reunited at the altar tomorrow. To be honest, though, I had my doubts about his abilities to stay away. I was prepared to get a three a.m. phone call asking me to come home so he could sleep.

Instead of a swanky dinner at a fancy restaurant that served five one-bite courses that I'd never be able to identify, relaxing in pajamas with takeout sounded heavenly. "You know what I'd really like?" I teased, lifting my eyebrows to taunt her.

Ellie leaned closer, obviously hoping my line of thinking was something naughty, like a strip club. "What?"

"To go to your place—our old place—order pizza, drink wine, and catch up on girl talk. Don't hate me because I know you pulled a miracle to get us dinner reservations at that swanky bistro . . . but I kind of just feel like staying in . . ."

She laughed. "I love that you're cool with eating pizza the night before your wedding and you're not on some crazy juice fast."

"Hell no. Either the dress fits or it doesn't. And Ben doesn't love me for the size on my tags."

She smiled. "You guys are too fuckin' cute for me to handle. It's a deal, as long as this girl talk includes you spilling some secrets on your fiancé's big dick and his skills in the bedroom."

I grinned devilishly. "For that, we'll need tequila instead of wine."

"Booyah. Let's go. We've got to stop on the way home for tequila." She smiled, grabbing my hand and hauling me from the office.

22

Ben

The moment I spotted Emmy advancing toward me down the center aisle, unshed tears in her eyes, I knew I'd love her forever. I could just picture us old and gray, sitting together telling stories of my modeling days and our adventures in Paris.

Seeing her walk down the aisle, watching the soft whoosh of her dress, the subtle sway of her hips, the tender way her hand rested on her father's forearm . . . all of it captivated me. But when she reached me at the altar I fought back a misty feeling forming behind my eyes. I'd never seen something so sweet. I couldn't imagine how someone so honest, so pure could love me for me. But Emmy did. Deeply. And I could see that reflected back at me from those gorgeous, bluish-gray eyes. She looked stunning. That was all I could focus on during the brief but loving ceremony, which was very Emmy. Simple yet elegant—and of course, genuine.

Now we were joined on the dance floor, surrounded by

our closest friends and relatives. I held her in my arms, swaying to the soulful melody played by the band. Life was perfect. My girl was mine. Forever.

Our families were getting along well; the only hitch came
when Emmy's mom spotted my mother's date. I thought her
eyeballs were going to fall out of her head when she saw the
guy my mom had brought to the reception. The guy couldn't
have been over twenty-five. Oh well.

I rarely heard anything about Fiona. Only that her baby
girl had been born. A little thing she'd named Alice. I was
happy for her. She'd gotten what she so desperately wanted—
to be a mother. And her brand-new daughter kept her too
busy to interfere in our lives.

The change in our lifestyle had been nice. With Emmy
running the charity, not everything was about my modeling
career anymore. I was looking forward to all that lay ahead
for us, beginning with a month-long honeymoon in St. Barts.

"Ben," Emmy said as she threaded her fingers through the
hair at the back of my neck.

"Yeah, baby?" I bent lower to brush my lips past her ear.

"I want . . ." she paused, stopping herself.

"What?"

"Um, nothing."

"Tell me."

"Never mind. It's a bad idea."

She had me intrigued. I cocked an eyebrow, challenging
her to continue as her eyes fluttered to the floor. "Look at me."
Her gaze latched onto mine once again. "Tell me."

"I want you," she admitted softly.

"You'll have me later. Several times," I promised.

She whimpered softly, her fingers tightening in my locks. "I want you right now."

"Fuck, baby, you can't say things like that."

"I need you deep inside me, please," she begged softly, keeping her voice low so no one could overhear our conversation.

Shit, her great uncle Rudy was dancing just beside us, and I could see her father and brother standing at the bar, their eyes flitting over to me and Emmy every now and again.

"Take me somewhere private . . ." she whispered.

"Look at me," I commanded. Her eyes lifted to mine. "Will you be quiet and behave like a good wife while I fuck you?"

A little groan tumbled from her parted pink lips and she quickly nodded.

I knew it was a bad idea, but my dick sprang to life on the dance floor, forcing me to tow her from the reception hall.

I laced her fingers between mine, loving the feel of the diamond ring brushing the inside of my hand. With one hand at the small of her back, I led her down a quiet hallway. At this time of night the hotel was all but deserted. I didn't know where I was taking her—a coat closet, an unoccupied office—but I settled for a women's restroom tucked down a seldom-used hallway in the back of the hotel.

Turning her to face me, I captured her mouth in a hungry kiss and used my back to push open the bathroom door, walking us backward through the doorway. Emmy's hands were instantly at my belt, making a tiny groan rumble in my chest. I loved knowing how badly she wanted me.

"Ben, I need you," Emmy whined.

"I know, baby. I want to fuck you so bad." How the fuck would I get her out of this dress? Since I had no clue how I'd get her dress off her, I figured I'd have to take her with it on, a thought that made me rock-hard.

Emmy pulled me toward the stall at the end, stopping to point at something on the floor and giggled. "Look. There are panties on the floor."

"Looks like we weren't the only ones with this idea. Our romantic wedding makes panties drop."

I chuckled softly, spotting the pair of pink frilly panties that lay discarded in the center of the room.

After a moment's hesitation, Emmy asked, "Ellie? Is that you?"

What the hell?

I peered underneath the stall door and spotted a pair of men's black Italian loafers just like the ones I wore and a pair of silver strappy high-heeled sandals. Fucking Braydon. And Ellie. Now there was an odd pair. They fought like damn cats and dogs.

"Yeah, um, Braydon's just helping me, um, find my contact," Ellie said, her voice husky and uneven.

Emmy hesitated just a moment, her brow pinching in confusion. "You don't wear contacts."

I chuckled again. Fucking Braydon. He made panties drop, I'd give him that.

"Yes, but I'm thinking of starting and I wanted to be sure . . ." Ellie continued.

I was about to intervene, to tug Emmy from the room and give them the privacy they obviously desired, when Braydon's stern voice answered, "We'll be out in a few minutes."

"Got it. And we'll see you shortly," I said. Taking Emmy's hand, I pulled her from the room.

We needed to rejoin our reception and spend time with our friends and families. But Emmy's flushed pink cheeks and fluttering pulse told me she needed relief. And fuck, so did I.

"Shall we go back in and say goodnight to everyone?" I asked, hesitating with her outside the doors to the ballroom.

She nodded. "Yes, but let's make it quick."

Returning to our reception was the right thing to do, though all I wanted was to get her naked underneath me.

We enjoyed a few more dances, made all the more erotic by our aroused state. When I couldn't stand the desperate look in Emmy's eyes any longer, we said our good-byes and I led her to the elevators.

Once inside the elevator, I punched the button for the floor to our suite. Circling one hand around the back of her neck, I latched her mouth to mine. By the time the elevator rolled to a stop her breathing was hard and ragged.

"This way."

She didn't speak. She just placed her hand on my arm and followed me.

Pushing open the door to our honeymoon suite, I removed my jacket, tossing it over an armchair in the opulent living room.

"Come here," I commanded, my voice low.

Emmy's eyes danced on mine as she crossed the room toward me.

I bent to one knee and raised her dress from the floor, lightly trailing my fingertips over her smooth calves. I removed each high-heeled shoe, certain she was ready to be done wearing them, even though they were sexy as fuck and she'd look stunning wearing nothing but them.

I rose to my feet and stood before her. "On your knees, Mrs. Shaw."

A soft whimper tumbled from her parted lips and she obeyed, lowering herself to her knees in front of me. Pretty gray eyes watched mine as her fingers fumbled to open my pants. She gripped my dick through the fabric, making a tortured groan rumble in my chest.

Her eyes widened at the sound as she lowered my zipper and pulled down my pants and boxer briefs, allowing me to spring free. Emmy gripped my base and guided me into her open mouth. Her warmth closed around my tip and I let out a strangled moan.

"Shit," I cursed, pushing my fingers into her hair. I loved looking down to watch her pleasure me. The way she swirled her tongue and licked me up and down while cradling my balls in one hand, circling my shaft with the other, was fucking incredible. I pulled myself free from her mouth and took her hand to urge her up.

Emmy rose on shaking feet and blinked up at me.

"Turn around."

She obeyed and I set to work removing her dress, undoing all the tiny little buttons running down her spine. Finally her dress slid down her body and pooled at the floor around her feet.

"Step out of it." I took her hand and helped her. Emmy faced me, wearing just a little white lace thong and a matching strapless bra. I surveyed her up and down. Creamy smooth skin, full pink lips, generous swell of cleavage that rose and fell with her quick breaths.

I pushed down her bra, exposing her breasts. God, she had perfect tits. More than enough to fill my palms, and perky pink nipples. I thumbed one peak and lowered my mouth to tease the other. Emmy pushed her chest out, urging me on.

I slipped one hand into the edge of her panties, leaving them on, but pushed them aside to expose her gorgeous pussy. Sweeping the pad of my index finger over her clit, Emmy shuddered and gripped my bicep. I thrummed against her, keeping up the same rhythm with my fingers and my tongue against her nipples. Within moments, Emmy was coming apart, clawing at my shoulders for support and whimpering as she came.

I held her tightly through the little aftershocks pulsing through her body and pressed tender kisses all over her mouth and neck.

"Thank you," she murmured.

I almost laughed. She didn't need to thank me. Making her come was the highlight of my day.

Her eyes flitted from mine to the bedroom door across the suite.

If I took her to bed right now, we'd make love, probably twice, and then fall asleep. Today was by far the best day of my life. I wanted to take my time—I didn't want tonight to end.

I tucked myself back into my pants and then stroked her cheek with my knuckle. "I don't want to rush this. Will you join me in the hot tub for a bit?"

She nodded, biting her lip.

While Emmy changed I gathered the chilled bottle of champagne, two glasses, and decadent chocolate-covered strawberries I'd had sent up and brought them all out onto the terrace.

Removing the hot tub cover, I tested the water. Perfect.

I stripped out of my tux, socks, and boxers and climbed into the water to wait for Emmy.

She emerged moments later with her hair in a loose bun and a purple string bikini.

Why had she changed? We had our luggage here for our honeymoon because we were leaving tomorrow, but still.

"Who said you could wear a bathing suit?" I asked, taking her hand to help her into the water.

She gently splashed me. "This way you get to unwrap me like a present."

"Hmm, I like that idea." I reached for her. "C'mere."

She placed a warm, wet hand in mine and I pulled her across the bench seat until we were close enough to touch.

"You looked stunning today."

"You liked my dress?"

"I loved it. It was perfect."

"What was your favorite part about today?" she asked.

"Hmm, probably when I heard you read your vows to me in your sweet southern accent. I knew this was really happening and you would be mine."

She grinned at me. "Was there any doubt?"

I raised a dark brow at her. "You have broken up with me twice," I teased.

"Now you're stuck with me. Forever."

"And ever." I pulled her to my lap, unable to resist taking things further. Her tits were peeking out of the little bikini top in the most distracting way. I needed it off of her.

Guiding her mouth to mine with one hand on her cheek, my other hand went to the back of her neck to untie the strings to her top. Once I freed her of the top, the naughty little thing began writhing in my lap, thrusting her chest out to rub her nipples over my skin. She was so sexy when she took control like this. I loved her confidence.

Emmy's eyes flew to mine. She felt my arousal nudging against her. The thin bikini bottoms were the only bit of fabric between us and provided little in the way of a barrier.

"I want to get you pregnant," I whispered in her ear before giving the lobe a gentle bite.

Emmy's eyes met mine. "Are you serious?"

"Completely."

A slow, lazy smile overtook her mouth.

I moved aside her bikini bottoms and pushed one finger slowly inside her. She was soaking wet. I positioned her so that each thigh was beside mine and lifted her up to meet my erection while my eyes met hers.

I pushed inside, entering her slowly, letting her feel every hard inch of me invade her. I wouldn't rush tonight.

I watched her take me in, her breathing coming in quick pants and her eyes slipping closed.

"Open them," I growled.

Her pretty gray-blue gaze locked with mine and she began riding me slowly, swirling her hips and rubbing her chest against mine.

"Shit," I cursed, gripping her hips but letting her use me just how she wanted to.

She slid up and down my length, increasing her speed, and my head fell back against the side of the hot tub. She was too much.

"Emmy . . ." she needed to slow down or I was going to lose it. And there was no way I was finishing before her.

"I'm gonna . . ." she panted, arching her back. Her tight walls pulsed around me and her nails bit into my shoulders as she clung to me.

Pushing deeply into her one last time, I exploded, filling her as I came.

When we'd finished I cradled her in my arms, letting the warm water lull us into relaxation. I held her as our heartbeats slowed, lightly caressing her skin. "I love you, baby," I whispered, burying my face in the crook of her neck.

She pulled back a fraction to meet my eyes. "I love you, too," she murmured.

"I know you do. You make me feel like I can do anything, be anything. Like I'm whole. Thank you for loving me despite the millions of reasons not to."

"I've always loved you. Right from the very beginning, even when I knew I shouldn't."

I pushed the wet locks of hair back from her face to meet her eyes. "Good girl, Mrs. Shaw."

Emmy climbed from my lap, rearranging her bottoms but leaving her top floating in the water. I opened the champagne and poured us each a glass.

"Cheers." I raised my glass to hers.

"To?"

Hmm. I thought it over. "Sex in hot tubs. Dirty texts." I took her hand, lacing her fingers between mine. "And love without end."

A pretty smile uncurled on her lips and she clinked her glass to mine. "Sounds perfect to me."

Acknowledgments

I have to thank Heather Maven for her keen eye and incredibly honest feedback regarding this story. She helped transform it into something filled with much more angst, and all together better. Thank you to the dear Kylie Scott, fabulous author of new adult romance, who when I email her begging for a critique, always sets time aside to read my horrible first drafts. Thank you lovely.

My darling husband who wholeheartedly supports everything I do, thank you, baby, for listening so attentively when I complain about my characters misbehaving or my word count not cooperating, and understanding when I turn on the light in the middle of the night and begin frantically scribbling in my notebook. You're made of awesome.

Lots of love to all my fans, I am so grateful for your support, for reading the stories that flow from my head. You make this possible. Thank you isn't enough, but it's all I have. THANK YOU!!!!

To my super-agent, Jane Dystel, who has been with me since the very beginning. I'm grateful for all you do to advocate for me and my books. Thank you to my editor, Jhanteigh, and the entire team at Atria for working with me and so patiently answering question after question that I threw at you.

Thank you to Christine and Denise at Shh Mom's Reading who've been supporters of mine from day one. You guys go above and beyond with blog tours and keeping every last detail coordinated so I don't have to. You are truly professionals and I adore you. I'd also like to give a special shout-out to Flirty & Dirty Book Blog and the Rockstars of Romance; though I've been fortunate to receive great support from numerous blogs, these two stand out as major advocates and it's not gone unnoticed by me. Your support has been exceptional. It means the world to me, ladies! Thank you.

Thank you to my amazing family for standing by my side and always supporting what I do. My support network and friends, author Zoey Foster, Ellie, and my street team, Kendall's Kinky Cuties, thank you for always cheering me on.

Read on for a sneak peek at Braydon and
Ellie's story in the next Love by Design novel
by Kendall Ryan

All or Nothing

Available in eBook and Paperback from Atria Books in
September 2014

Ellie

"Ahhhhh..." A deep male groan broke from behind the closed door.

Sex noises seemed really out of place in a church. Call me old-fashioned, but I was certain of two things: One, doggie style should be reserved for the bedroom, and two, we were all going to hell. "Come on," I urged Braydon, tugging his tux-edo-clad elbow. "We can't listen to this."

"I'm not going anywhere." His feet remained planted to the floor, despite my efforts to shove him farther down the hall.

A loud, thundering moan vibrated from the other side of the door.

My eyes jerked up to Braydon's. His mouth quirked up in a lopsided grin, showing off his perfect dimple. He lowered himself to the floor, leaning his back against the wall with his long legs stretched out in front of him, and crossed his feet at the ankles.

"What are you doing?" I hissed. *Shouldn't we give our friends some privacy?*

"Guarding the door." He shrugged. "I'm sure one of those photographers outside would love a shot of the action in there." He gestured with a nod toward the door.

I couldn't argue with that. There was a fleet of paparazzi outside who'd give their left testicle to get a shot of the action today. This wedding was practically the event of the summer in Manhattan. World-famous male supermodel Ben Shaw's wedding my best friend, Emmy, would be front-page news on the celebrity gossip sites.

I looked down at Braydon's stretched-out form. He was dressed in a tailored black Armani tuxedo, crisp white shirt, and sleek Italian leather shoes that tapered just slightly at the toe. His bowtie was hanging loose around his open collar, and he was sipping from a silver flask, watching me curiously.

"Come sit with me." He tapped the floor beside him with his knuckles. "Those shoes can't be comfortable." His eyes slowly lowered, wandering the length of my black strapless gown and all the way down to my strappy five-inch heels.

He was right again; I'd been in them for thirty minutes and already I could feel my toes becoming numb. The price of beauty. Sometimes it sucked being a girl. I sighed, not wanting to admit he was right.

"I won't bite, kitten. Unless you want it rough." He flashed his dimpled grin at me again and my stomach knotted.

Braydon tested my willpower like no one else. I'd sworn off men, so why did I want to take off my panties and give in to him? Lord, this wasn't healthy. Not one bit. I forced my eyes from his. Gazing into his navy blue depths felt entirely too intimate. He saw too much. I wondered if he knew just how much he got my heart racing. I'd met him last year through our mutual friends, Ben and Emmy. He was a sinfully sexy male model, often working with Emmy's soon-to-be husband, and trouble with a capital T.

Defeated, I slipped off my heels and sunk down on the floor next to him. Trying to maintain a sense of modesty, I arranged heaps of black satin and organza around my legs in the hallway of the church where my best friend was about to wed the man of her dreams. Pity party, your table of one is now available. I knew it was cliché, but weddings depressed me. Always have. I'd helped Emmy into her dress and fussed with her veil until it was just perfect. And now, I could only imagine what was going on in that church library, and the mess I'd have to clean up before their wedding ceremony even began.

"Ben wanted a quick fuck." Braydon shrugged like this situation was completely normal.

Oh, that was romantic. Men were disgusting. I rolled my eyes at him, I felt like sticking out my tongue too, but I didn't. Weren't most people nervous before their wedding? Apparently Ben and Emmy were just horny.

But this was fucking ridiculous. Their wedding ceremony was scheduled to begin in twenty minutes, and I could see the stream of guests already filtering in and sitting with the assistance of the ushers. When Ben had come knocking at the door, looking for Emmy, I hadn't argued, I'd just helped her out of the one-of-a-kind white lace gown made just for her by Vera Wang, and let him inside the little library where we'd been getting ready.

His eyes had drunk her in, moving down from the little white bra and panty set to the pale blue garter around her thigh. "Fuck, sweetheart," he'd murmured.

The chemistry and intensity between them was impossible to ignore. It'd always been that way between them though. Ben had crossed the room in three long strides, stopping in front of her and watching her with a look of adoration. His hands had skated down her sides, gliding over her hips and thighs. His voice had been a weak whisper when he told her how beautiful she looked. My heart had twisted in my chest. It was obvious how much he loved her, despite how many times he'd messed up. You only found a love like that once in a lifetime. And as happy as I was that my best friend had found it, it only reminded me of how painfully alone I was.

As I sat trying not to listen to my friends go at it in the tiny church library, I wished it was me in that room with a white poufy dress pushed up to my ears as a man who was so deeply in love with me couldn't wait another moment to be inside me.

"Is it true?" he asked, passing me the flask.

"Is what true?" I accepted it and took a small sip. Mmm. I wasn't expecting it to taste good. Citrus vodka. My favorite.

"That bridesmaids are horny at weddings," he chuckled.

"Guess you'll have to be a good boy tonight to find out," I replied, taking a healthy swig from the flask before handing it back to him. "Zoey and Jenna are both single." So was I, but that wasn't happening. No thanks. I'd be leaving here to tonight with my dignity intact.

His eyes lifted to mine. "There's someone else I had in mind, actually."

That little pang of nerves in my stomach was back. He needed to stop flirting with me. I wasn't interested. Sure, my body processed that he was sexy—he was a supermodel for goodness sake—but my brain wasn't stupid enough to fall for his batting eyelashes and quips. I wasn't going to be another notch on his belt. "That's not happening," I deadpanned.

Braydon chuckled, the low rasp sliding from his perfect lips. He was like one of those jock-types in high school who thought the V on his varsity jacket stood for vagina. He was a total player, I was sure of it. "We'll see," he said.

"I'm a bitch to you. Why do you even like me?" I asked.

"I don't argue with my cock, sweetheart. And he seems to like you. In fact, he'd like to get to know you a lot better."

Good Lord! He couldn't say things like that to me. I wanted to tell him where to take his cock and shove it, but I was afraid of what might come out of my mouth.

His hand patted mine. It was meant to calm me, but any time he touched me little darts of heat fractured out from his fingertips and across my skin. It was disorienting. I pulled my hand away and tucked it safely into my lap.

We sat there in silence, passing the flask back and forth, listening to our friends' muted sex noises. God, it'd been entirely too long since I'd gotten any. I clamped my thighs together and groaned. I felt Braydon watching me and turned to meet his eyes.

"You need something, kitten?" His voice was deep and low. Too sexy for his own good.

"I'm fine," I squeaked out. "You good?"

"Oh, I'm fucking fantastic."

Finally, the door opened and Ben emerged, his hair thoroughly rumpled—from Emmy's wandering hands, no doubt. A giant smile was planted across his full mouth.

I rolled my eyes. "You two need to go. I need to get her dressed." I gestured to Braydon. "Go fix his sex hair."

Braydon saluted me. "You got it, boss."

The wedding ceremony was beautiful and heartfelt, perfectly representative of Ben and Emmy, just as I knew it would be. They had written their own vows and exchanged them in a tearful display in front of several hundred guests. It was beautiful to watch.

After a thousand photos and makeup touch-ups, we arrived at the reception at a beautiful, historic hotel overlooking Central Park. They'd certainly gotten lucky today. August in New York City could be brutally hot and humid, but today was mild, sunny, and perfect.

All through pictures, dinner, drinks, and dancing, I played the perfect maid of honor. I was attentive to Emmy, smiled and made small talk with her loopy relatives from Tennessee, danced with her rather sweaty cousin, Randy Joe, and was fondled by her perverted Uncle Lou more than once.

I'd lied and told Emmy I was fine not having a date to her wedding—I'd reasoned that being the maid of honor meant I'd be too busy to entertain a man. But the truth was, watching Ben hold Emmy close on the dance floor and seeing the older couples swaying together made me realize it was pointless to lie to myself. Not that I had any viable date options. My recent prospects consisted solely of a string of lousy first dates, thanks to the Internet, with no real prospects on the horizon. My best friend's wedding only amplified my loner status. *Enter shame spiral.*

I wanted that deep, all-consuming love and acceptance when someone just got you. I didn't just want a boyfriend. I craved true intimacy and the peace of knowing I'd found "my someone." I was tired of the game, and I wanted to settle down with a nice man. But something told me working sixty hours a week as a scientist and shunning the entire male population wouldn't make it easy to find my happily ever after. I wasn't foolish enough to believe in fairy tales, but having a front-row seat to my best friend falling in love with a male model, traveling the world, and gushing about mind-blowing sex with a man who was allegedly hung like a baby elephant, was making me hold out hope for my own Prince Charming. Possibly to my own detriment.

With my high heels pinching my feet, I headed for the exit, needing a moment to myself. The dance floor raged behind me, but my destination was one of quiet solitude. Emmy's mom stopped me in my path.

"Darling, I think we're low on champagne. There's more in the storage closet down the hall. Would you mind?"

"Not at all." It'd give me a reason to escape for a few minutes. Be alone and catch my breath.

"I'll escort her." Braydon appeared beside me out of nowhere. I'd noticed him throughout the night, quietly sipping his beer and keeping me in his sights but maintaining his distance.

His tone and the intense look in his eyes left little room for argument, so I merely nodded and turned for the exit. Making my way through the crowded ballroom, I felt Braydon's hand ghosting along the small of my back as he guided me. Little flutters of heat raced down my spine, pooling low in my belly. I turned down the deserted hallway, thankful for a moment of silence. Today had been exhausting. Not to mention it wasn't the easiest thing in the world to be surrounded by two people who were so in love when my own love life was in the crapper.

We reached the storage room at the end of a long hallway only to find it locked.

"Dammit," I muttered, wrenching on the door handle.

"It's fine. We'll just find one of the catering staff and ask them to bring up more champagne." His hand closed around my elbow and an electric current zapped through me. It was as though his body knew mine and was calling to me. *What the hell was that?*

"Hey," Braydon said, lifting my chin to his. "Is everything okay?"

"Fine," I lied. "Why?"

He lifted one shoulder. "You don't seem like yourself. Tonight, after that speech . . . I don't know. I wondered where my little firecracker had gone . . ." His hand lifted to my upper arm and glided along my skin in slow, measured strokes.

He was incredibly perceptive. Too much so. But I couldn't have him getting to me. My maid of honor speech had been cut short when a lump of emotion had lodged in my throat, and I'd nearly broken down in front of everyone. I'd said a quick congratulations and ended it. Emmy and Ben seemed none the wiser, happily kissing and clinking their champagne glasses. I found it interesting that Braydon, of all people, had been perceptive enough to pick up on the change in me.

I sucked in a fortifying breath. I couldn't let him see how weak and alone I felt. "She's still here and will happily kick you in the balls if you decide to get too handsy." I glared at the hand he'd left resting on my bare shoulder.

He quickly withdrew the offending hand. "Glad you're back."

I swallowed down a wave of nerves, my heartbeat quickening as I realized we were all alone.

"You look stunning tonight. I should have told you earlier," he said.

My eyes lifted to his and I parted my lips to speak, to give him one of the sassy quips I was known for, but nothing came out.

"Shh, it's okay," he said, his palm cupping my cheek. "You don't have to be tough all the time, you know?"

I nodded slowly.

"I know you can take care of yourself, but who takes care of you, Ellie?"

He rarely, if ever, called me by my actual name, and the familiarity of it passing over his lips caused a little ripple of desire to dance in my belly. "No one," I admitted. "Men suck."

"I can't argue with that. Most men are assholes who behave like spoiled children."

I nodded slowly, glad we were on the same page. I thought he'd try to convince me otherwise, or at least tell me that he wasn't one of them. But he just stayed quiet, watching me with those gorgeous blue eyes of his, making my skin hum with nervous anticipation. *What were we doing?*

"I could take care of you tonight, make you feel good, if you let me," he whispered, his mouth just a few inches from mine.

My heart rioted in my chest. He was so good-looking, so sexy. I knew it'd be incredible. But the word *tonight* stood out to me. I was done with men who wanted one night with me. I supposed a string of failed dates and one-night-stands would do that to you. I was looking for something more. A deeper, intimate connection; a real relationship. Not a one-night stand, not a guy who wanted nothing to do with me in the morning. Braydon had a way with words, I'd give him that. That didn't mean anything was going to happen, though.

"A few sexy words and you expect me to just hand over my panties?" I quipped.

"No. I'd prefer to peel those off you myself. Slowly. Savoring every delicious inch of skin I exposed."

My eyes slipped closed. My body was screaming at me to give in, to pull him into the nearest coat closet or restroom and let him have his way with me. To make this ache between my thighs go away. But my brain, ever in control, knew I couldn't do that.

"May I kiss you?" he whispered.

Temptation to kiss him flared inside me, unbidden and unwelcome. I'd been unconsciously watching the way his mouth moved when he spoke, as he took sips from his glass, fantasizing about how those full lips would feel against mine. Despite my body's urgings, I slowly shook my head.

"What are you afraid of?" he whispered. "Falling for me?"

I raised an eyebrow, looking at him like he'd grown a second head. "There's no chance of that happening," I scoffed.

"Then kiss me," he rasped.

"Why would I kiss you?" I asked, breathless yet fighting to remain in control.

"Because you want to." His statement was bold, direct, and sure. I hated how well he could read me.

"No, I don't," I murmured weakly. *Stay strong, Ellie.*

He chuckled softly. "Okay, kitten. Then let me kiss you. I want to see if you're still as feisty when that pretty mouth is occupied."

My silence was the only answer he needed.

He took my hand and dragged me the few paces to the

women's restroom across the hall. In this quiet part of the hotel, it was deserted.

Braydon's warm palm cupped the bare nape of my neck, his thumb lightly rubbing against the soft skin. A chill darted down my spine. The simple contact from his hand was more than enough to ignite the fireworks between us into a raging inferno. His touch was firm, knowing, and decidedly confident.

With his hand still planted firmly at the base of my neck, he guided my body to his until our chests rested together. Our hearts pounded against each other, and I didn't know if it was from the adrenaline surge of arguing with him or the desire I felt flooding my system.

He certainly knew how to make my heart race.

All the bickering and heated arguments gave way to this moment. His blue eyes gazed fiercely down at mine and my tongue unconsciously darted out to wet my bottom lip. Braydon didn't miss the movement, his own lips parting as he softly inhaled.

I had no idea what he saw in me—what he must think of me—with my razor-sharp tongue and the neon sign above my head advertising how much I distrusted men. But in this moment, he obviously didn't care. He was every bit as wrapped up in this as I was. Maybe he was just horny, maybe it was our roles as maid of honor and best man at our best friends' wedding that had brought us to this moment . . . but regardless, there was no denying I wanted him to kiss me.

He was the king of mixed signals. He'd poked fun at me all day, and now he was looking like he wanted to devour me from the inside out. The thought made my stomach flip. With my chest brushing his, I felt my nipples harden beneath my satin gown. I wasn't sure if he felt it too, but Braydon's eyes grew dark with his desire and began to slip closed. I didn't know what to make of him, but before I could even begin to sort out my feelings, his lips pressed tenderly against mine.

The softness in his kiss was unexpected. His fingers curled around my neck, fastening my mouth to his while he demanded I give in.

Knowing we were tucked away, with no chance of being discovered, I gave in to my desires. His fingers slowly knotted in my hair as he pulled me closer and deepened the kiss, his tongue lightly probing my mouth.

He was too sure. Too skilled. My libido immediately took notice, delivering a healthy dose of moisture to my panties. He turned something as simple as a kiss into a promise for sweaty, heart-pounding sex. If he kissed this well, surely he would be commanding and confident in the bedroom. Why did that thought excite me so much? I kissed him back with everything I had, my tongue sliding intimately against his as I tangled my hands in his hair.

After several moments, he slowly broke away, grinning against my mouth. "That wasn't so bad, was it?"

I parted my lips and drew a slow, shaky breath. I wanted

to beg him to kiss me again, but instead I lifted one shoulder then dropped it in a noncommittal shrug. "It was okay."

He tipped his head back and laughed out loud. "You're lying. I can see your body's response to me, kitten. Your panties are probably wet right now. Just from that one kiss."

I didn't deny it—I just held my eyes on his. Even in these insanely high heels, I had to tilt my head up to look up at him. He evoked strange responses from my body. One minute I wanted to bite his head off for being a player, and the next I wanted to mount him and make him show me just how experienced he was between the sheets. God, I should be checked for multiple personalities. *Hold it together, Ellie!*

He bent down and his hands disappeared under the hem of my dress, skimming up my naked calves and thighs. Chill bumps broke out in the wake of his smooth hands roaming along my skin. Was he honestly going to check if my panties were wet? And was I seriously going to let him? I knew I should stop him, slap his hands away, step back—something—but instead I stood there like a lovesick idiot, letting him manhandle me.

His fingers slid in through the sides of my panties and slowly twisted them, pulling them down my thighs. I knew I should say something. This wasn't okay, this wasn't me. Yet I watched in wonder as he let them fall to my ankles.

"Step out of them," he commanded.

I lifted one foot and then the other, leaving my panties lying haphazardly on the floor.

He slid one finger against my sex, and his mouth curved up in a grin. "You get really wet, don't you?"

Heat flooded my cheeks and my eyes dropped to the floor. *Oh, God.*

He tipped my chin up to meet his eyes once again. "Fuck, I like that. A lot."

I pulled in a shaky breath, relaxing into his touch.

His finger glided along my wet center and a whimper fell from my parted lips. It was laced with need, and Braydon recognized it immediately, his jaw tightening. His eyes danced as he looked into mine, and we tried to calm our ragged breathing.

"All this tension between us, my little firecracker, this electricity . . . don't you want to see what it will be like when I'm buried balls-deep inside you?" he murmured, his finger lightly rubbing my clit as his eyes met mine. I whimpered and bit my lip. Braydon continued watching me as though cataloging my every reaction as his finger continued to carefully circle the bundle of nerve endings so desperate for attention.

God, if he keeps that up, I'm going to explode . . .

"Can I taste you?" he asked.

All the blood rushed from my brain to my clenching sex, and I nodded wordlessly.

Walking us backward, Braydon guided me into one of the large bathroom stalls and slid the clasp into place, locking the door behind us. My heart pounded in anticipation.

Our eyes connected as he lowered himself to his knees in front of me, pushing my dress up around my hips as he went.

Raw desire was reflected back at me as those beautiful blue depths penetrated mine. He hungered to put his mouth on me, and that thought alone drove me absolutely wild.

Balancing on precariously high heels with a poufy satin dress lifted up around my waist, I braced one hand on the wall beside me for support.

"Put your hands here." He took my wrists, placing my hands on his shoulders instead. Then he slowly leaned forward, planting sweet kisses along my inner thigh. I writhed, trying to push myself closer, and balled my fists into his shirt.

"Hang on baby. I'll take care of you. I promise."

His words instantly soothed me. I knew they would.

What in the world was happening between me and Braydon? I had no clue. But hell if I wanted to stop it. His tantalizing mouth moved to my other thigh, giving it the same treatment, trailing tender, sucking kisses all over the smooth flesh.

I gripped his shirt, my fingers sliding from his shoulders to his collar to his hair, using it to tug him closer.

"Okay, enough teasing," he whispered. "You want to come?"

"Yes," I groaned out.

His mouth closed over my sex, sucking my swollen flesh into his mouth. He certainly wasn't shy. This wasn't the timid, noncommittal technique I was used to from most guys—a few flicks of the tongue before retreating to check a box. *Oral sex complete*. No, Braydon invested himself fully, pinning me in place and worshipping my lady parts until I was moaning and tugging against his hair to get him to ease up.

Hushed voices and footsteps came within hearing range. Braydon didn't stop his ministrations, despite me trying to wiggle away. His hands clamped down on my hips, holding me in place. The footsteps stopped just beside the door, and I peeked one eye open. I could see black Italian loafers and hot pink satin pumps under the doorway. *Holy shit!* It was Ben and Emmy.